SUMMER CAMP SCIENCE MYSTERIES

#3 The **Hunt** for **Hidden** **Treasure**

A Mystery about Rocks

by Lynda Beauregard

illustrated by Guillermo Mogorrón

GRAPHIC UNIVERSE™ • MINNEAPOLIS • NEW YORK

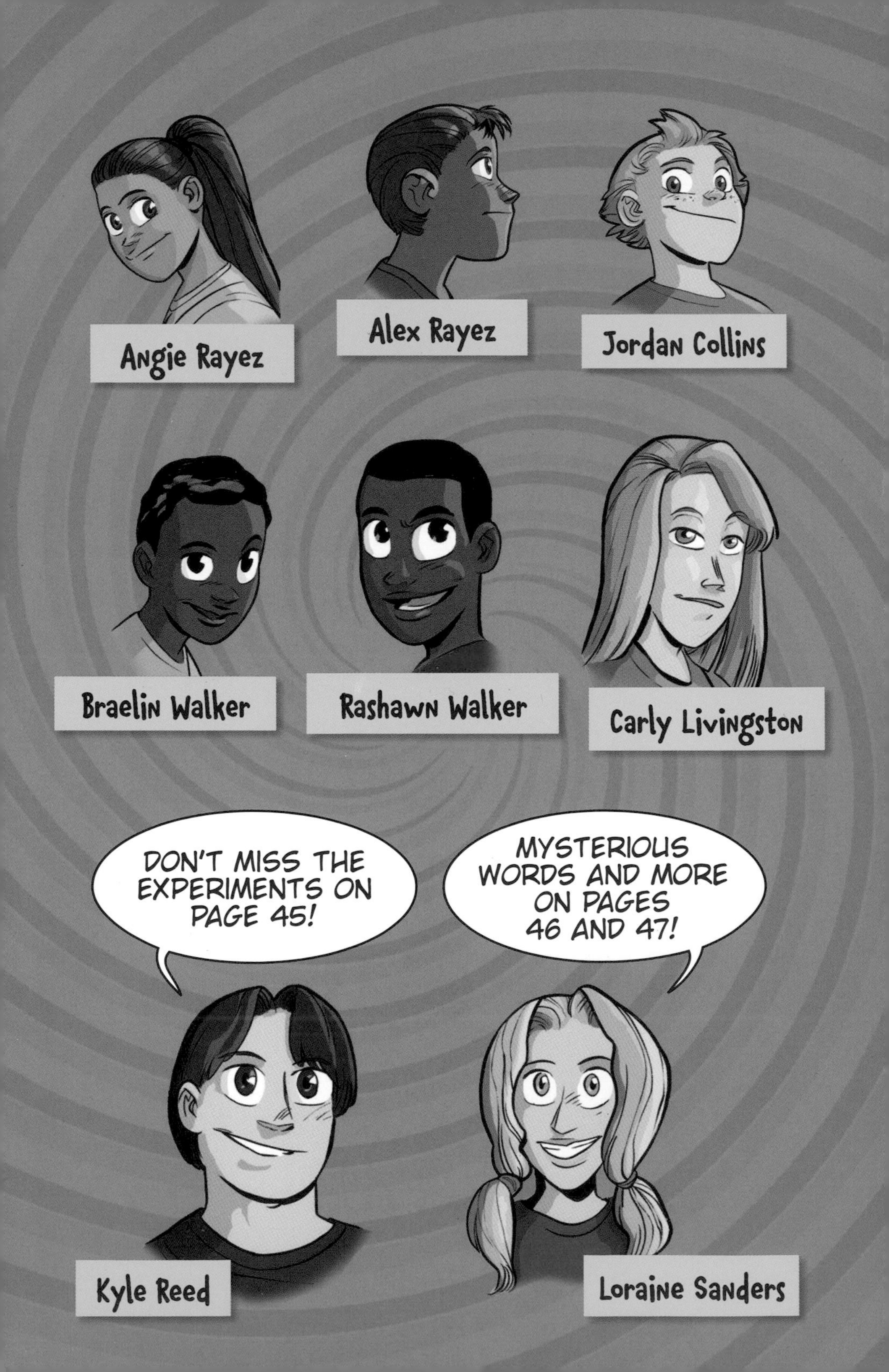
Angie Rayez
Alex Rayez
Jordan Collins
Braelin Walker
Rashawn Walker
Carly Livingston
DON'T MISS THE EXPERIMENTS ON PAGE 45!
MYSTERIOUS WORDS AND MORE ON PAGES 46 AND 47!
Kyle Reed
Loraine Sanders

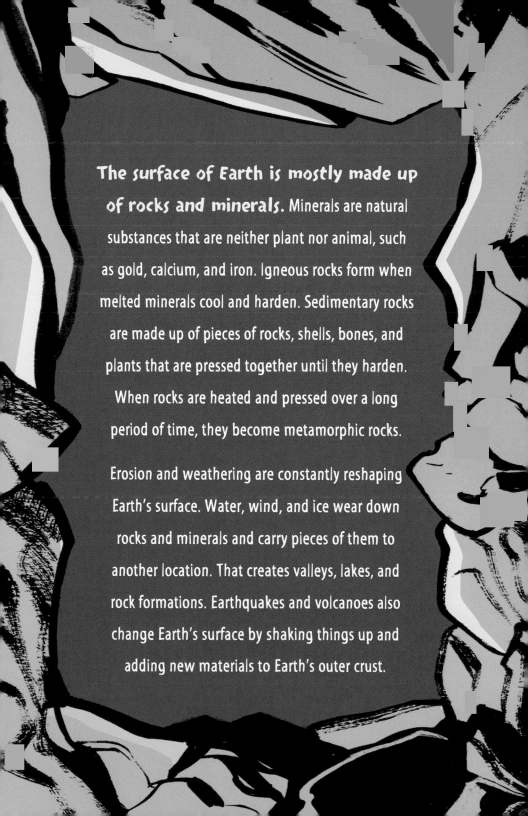

**The surface of Earth is mostly made up of rocks and minerals.** Minerals are natural substances that are neither plant nor animal, such as gold, calcium, and iron. Igneous rocks form when melted minerals cool and harden. Sedimentary rocks are made up of pieces of rocks, shells, bones, and plants that are pressed together until they harden. When rocks are heated and pressed over a long period of time, they become metamorphic rocks.

Erosion and weathering are constantly reshaping Earth's surface. Water, wind, and ice wear down rocks and minerals and carry pieces of them to another location. That creates valleys, lakes, and rock formations. Earthquakes and volcanoes also change Earth's surface by shaking things up and adding new materials to Earth's outer crust.

Story by Lynda Beauregard
Pencils and inks by Guillermo Mogorrón
Coloring by John Novak
Lettering by Grace Lu

Graphic Universe™
A division of Lerner Publishing Group, Inc.
241 First Avenue North
Minneapolis, MN 55401 U.S.A.

Website address: www.lernerbooks.com

Main body text set in CCWildwords.
Typeface provided by Comicraft/Active Images.

Library of Congress Cataloging-in-Publication Data

Beauregard, Lynda.
    The hunt for hidden treasure : a mystery about rocks / by Lynda Beauregard ; illustrated by Guillermo Mogorrón.
        p.   cm. — (Summer camp science mysteries, #3)
    ISBN: 978–0–7613–5690–5 (lib. bdg. : alk. paper)
    1. Graphic novels. [1. Graphic novels. 2. Camps—Fiction. 3. Geology—Fiction.]
I. Mogorrón, Guillermo, 1978– ill. II. Title.
PZ7.7.B42Hu 2012
741.5'973—dc23                                           2011022375

Manufactured in the United States of America
1 – CG – 12/31/11

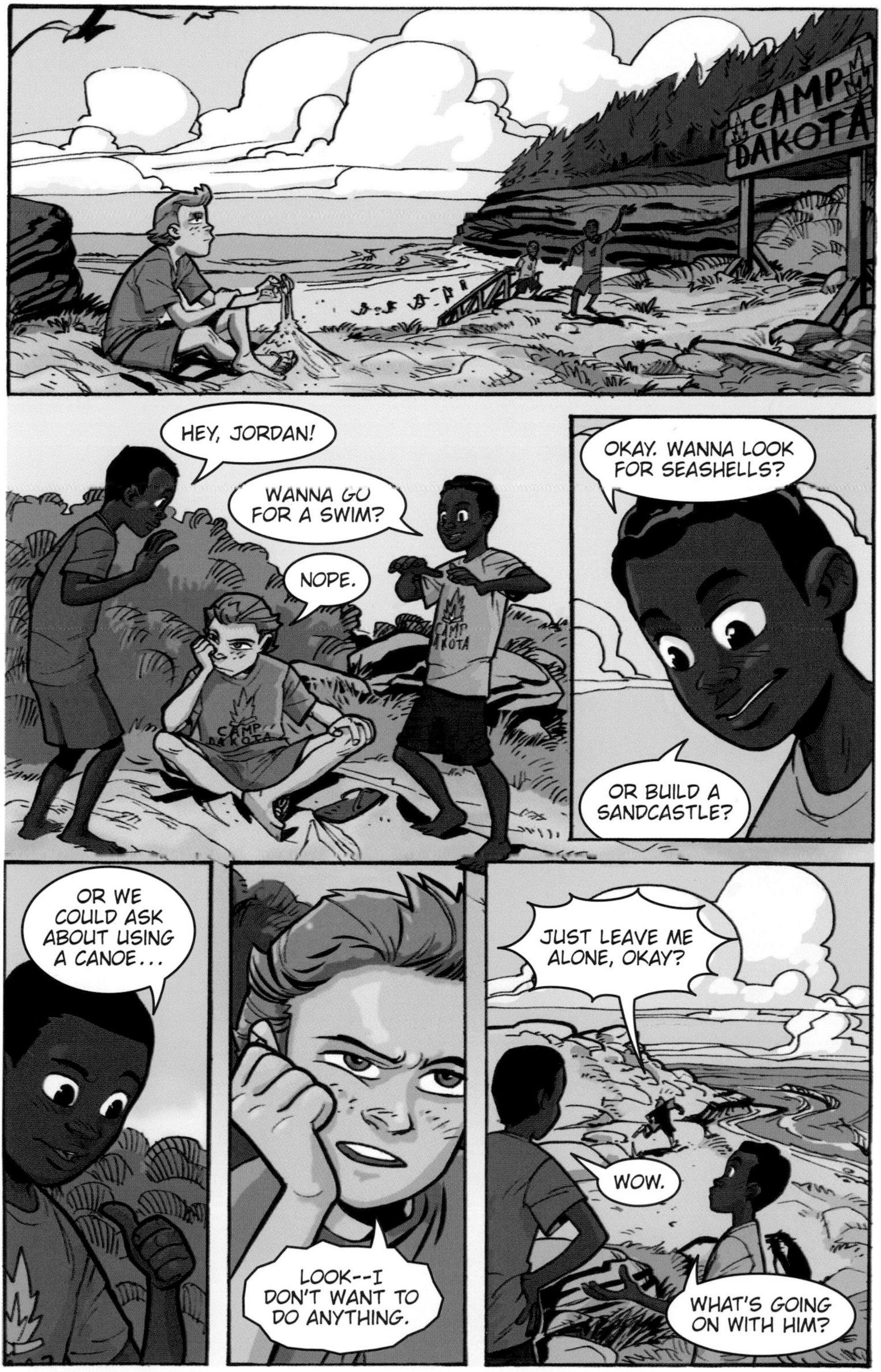
CAMP DAKOTA
HEY, JORDAN!
WANNA GO FOR A SWIM?
NOPE.
OKAY. WANNA LOOK FOR SEASHELLS?
OR BUILD A SANDCASTLE?
OR WE COULD ASK ABOUT USING A CANOE...
LOOK--I DON'T WANT TO DO ANYTHING.
JUST LEAVE ME ALONE, OKAY?
WOW.
WHAT'S GOING ON WITH HIM?

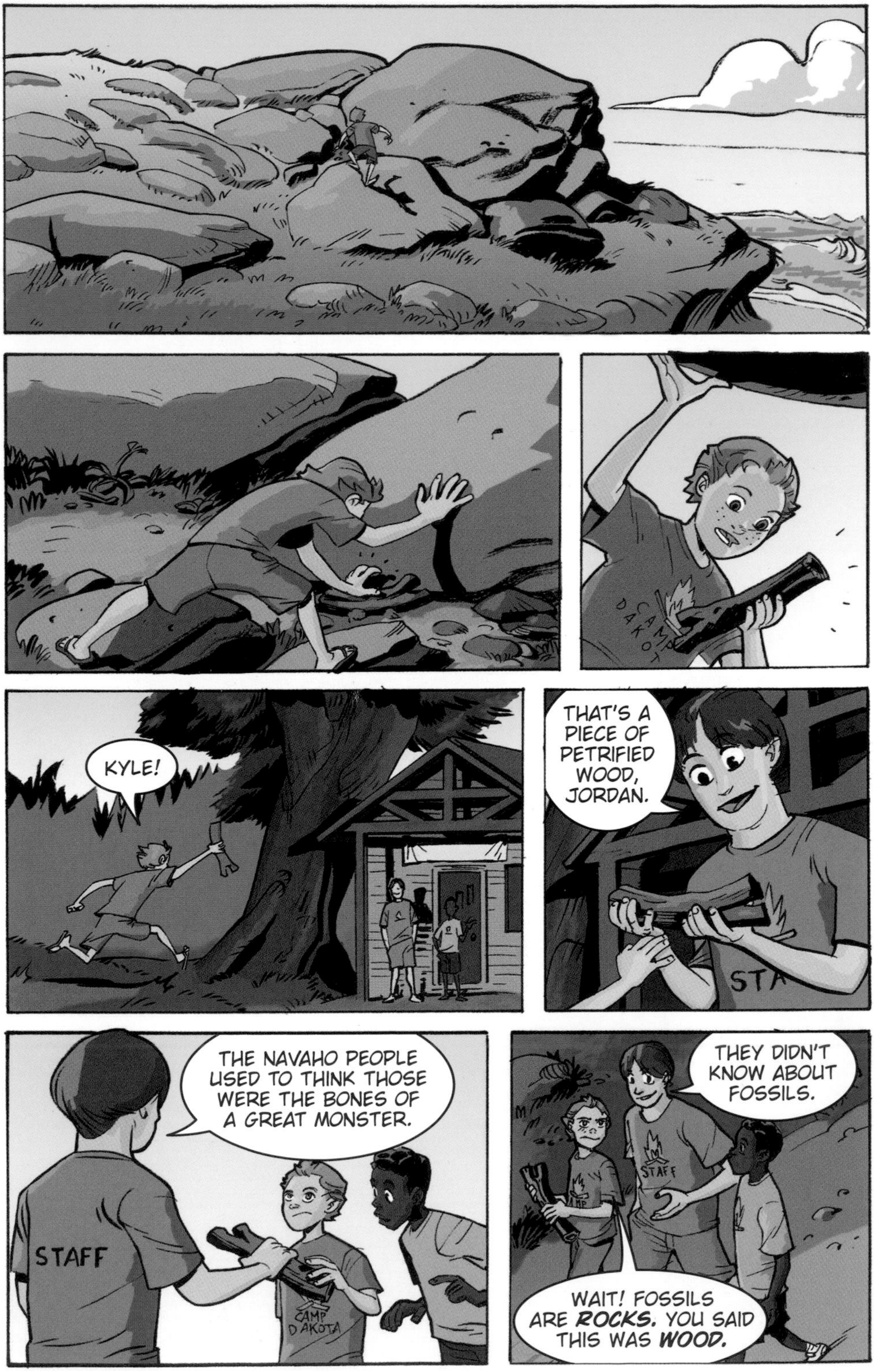
CAMP DAKOTA
KYLE!
THAT'S A PIECE OF PETRIFIED WOOD, JORDAN.
STA
STAFF
THE NAVAHO PEOPLE USED TO THINK THOSE WERE THE BONES OF A GREAT MONSTER.
CAMP DAKOTA
THEY DIDN'T KNOW ABOUT FOSSILS.
STAFF
WAIT! FOSSILS ARE **ROCKS.** YOU SAID THIS WAS **WOOD.**

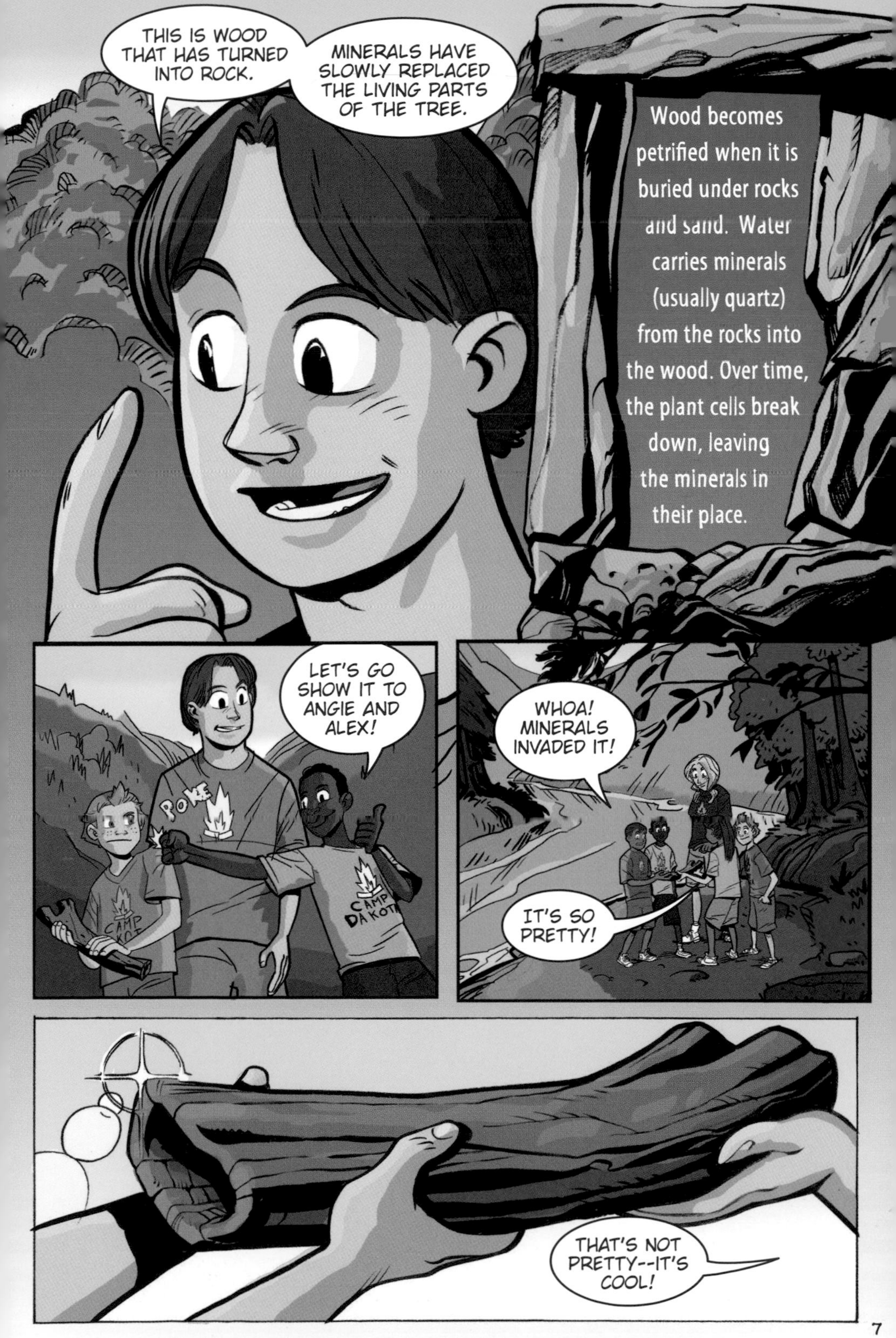
THIS IS WOOD THAT HAS TURNED INTO ROCK.
MINERALS HAVE SLOWLY REPLACED THE LIVING PARTS OF THE TREE.
Wood becomes petrified when it is buried under rocks and sand. Water carries minerals (usually quartz) from the rocks into the wood. Over time, the plant cells break down, leaving the minerals in their place.
LET'S GO SHOW IT TO ANGIE AND ALEX!
POKE
CAMP DAKOTA
WHOA! MINERALS INVADED IT!
IT'S SO PRETTY!
THAT'S NOT PRETTY--IT'S COOL!

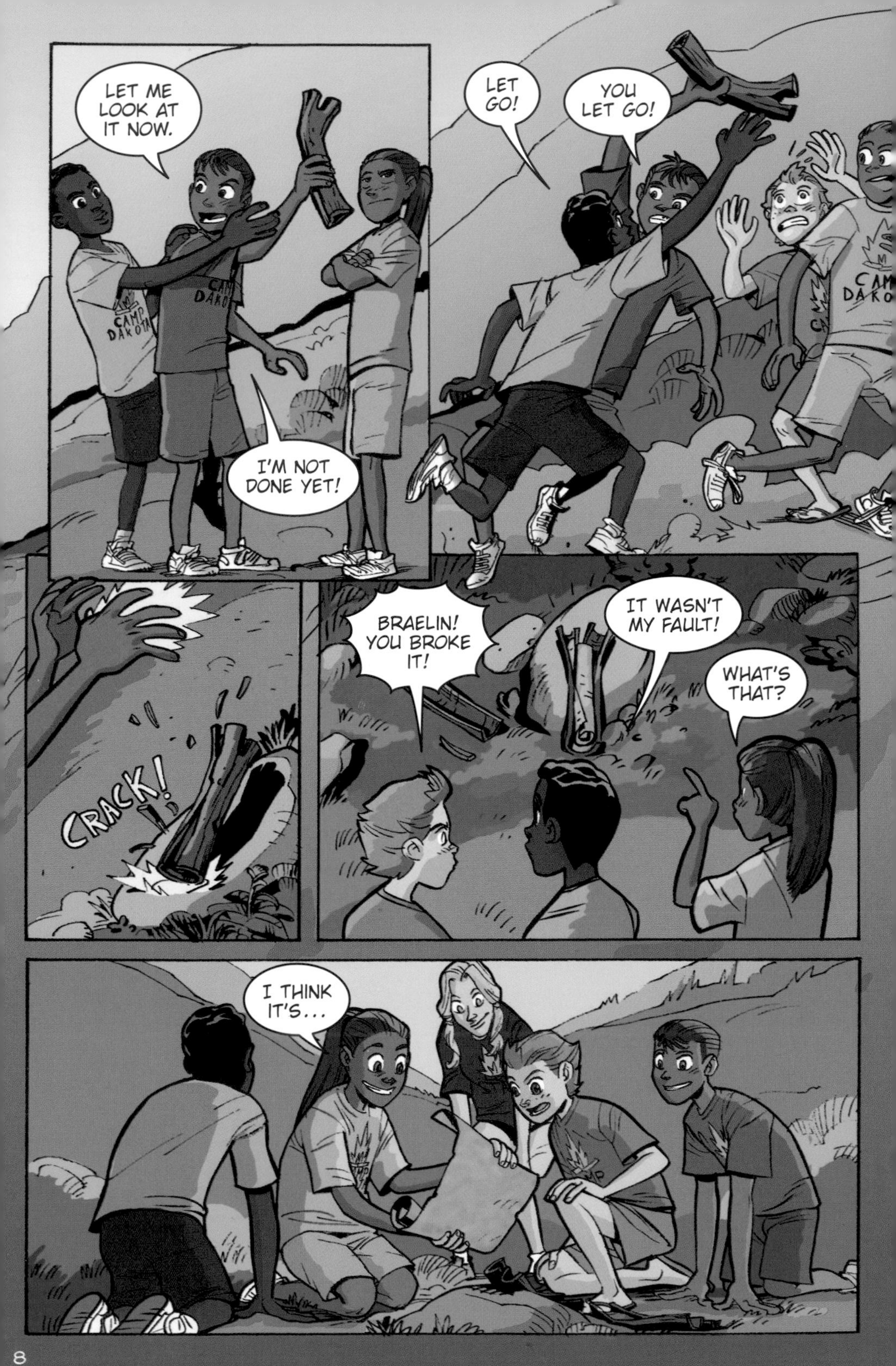
LET ME LOOK AT IT NOW.
I'M NOT DONE YET!
LET GO!
YOU LET GO!
CRACK!
BRAELIN! YOU BROKE IT!
IT WASN'T MY FAULT!
WHAT'S THAT?
I THINK IT'S...

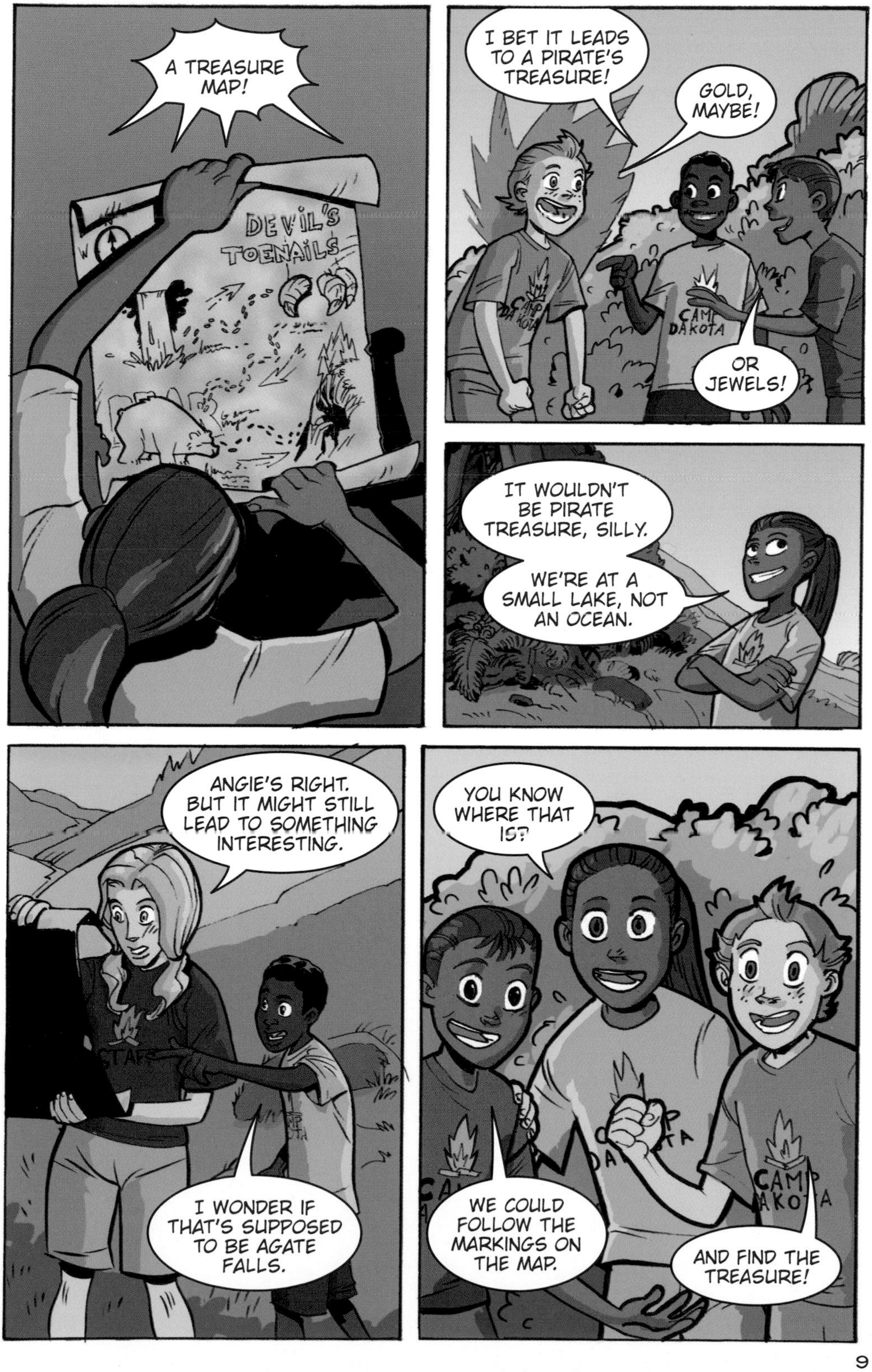
A TREASURE MAP!
DEVIL'S TOENAILS
I BET IT LEADS TO A PIRATE'S TREASURE!
GOLD, MAYBE!
OR JEWELS!
IT WOULDN'T BE PIRATE TREASURE, SILLY.
WE'RE AT A SMALL LAKE, NOT AN OCEAN.
ANGIE'S RIGHT. BUT IT MIGHT STILL LEAD TO SOMETHING INTERESTING.
I WONDER IF THAT'S SUPPOSED TO BE AGATE FALLS.
YOU KNOW WHERE THAT IS?
WE COULD FOLLOW THE MARKINGS ON THE MAP.
AND FIND THE TREASURE!

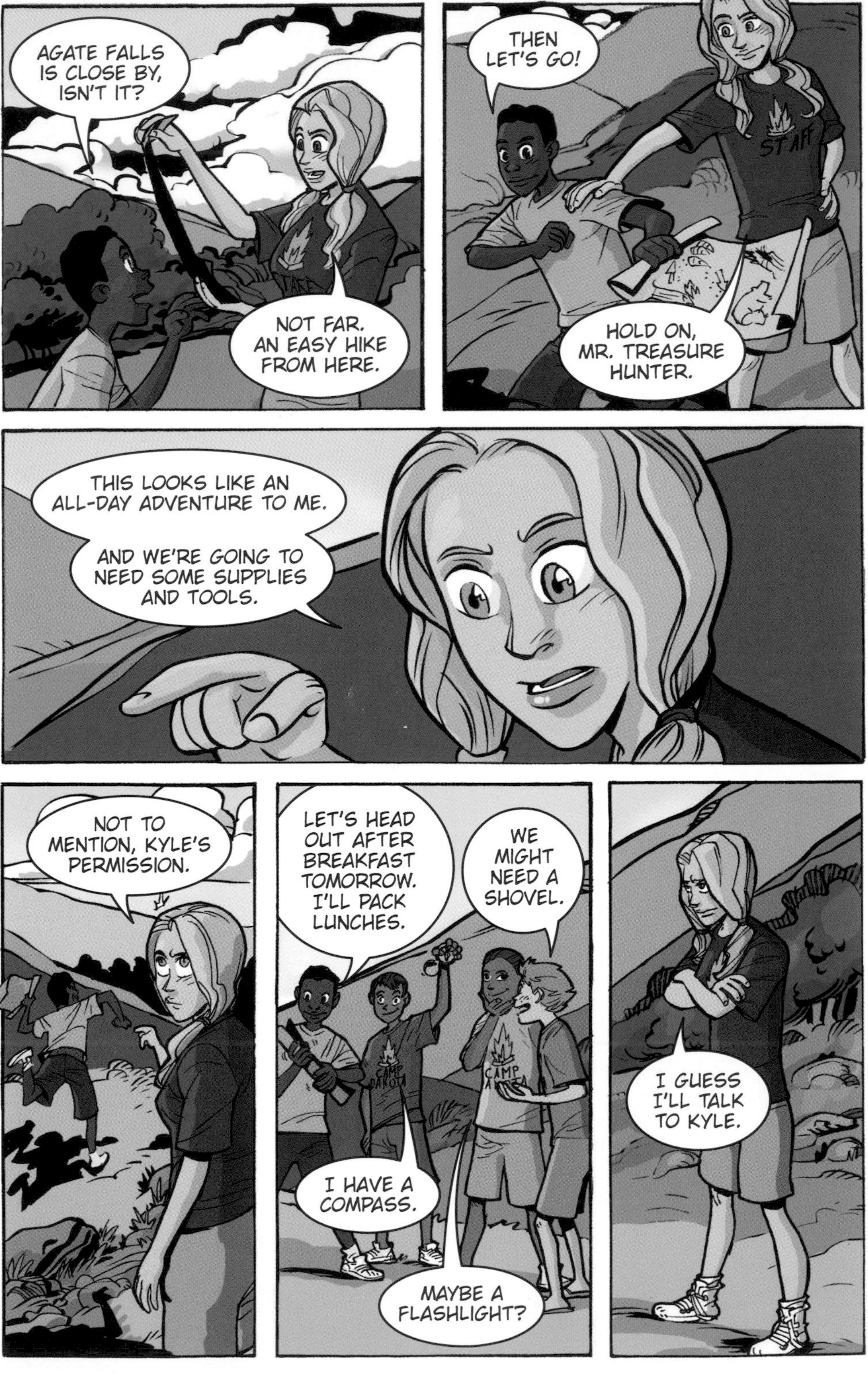
AGATE FALLS IS CLOSE BY, ISN'T IT?
NOT FAR. AN EASY HIKE FROM HERE.
THEN LET'S GO!
HOLD ON, MR. TREASURE HUNTER.
THIS LOOKS LIKE AN ALL-DAY ADVENTURE TO ME.
AND WE'RE GOING TO NEED SOME SUPPLIES AND TOOLS.
NOT TO MENTION, KYLE'S PERMISSION.
LET'S HEAD OUT AFTER BREAKFAST TOMORROW. I'LL PACK LUNCHES.
WE MIGHT NEED A SHOVEL.
I HAVE A COMPASS.
MAYBE A FLASHLIGHT?
I GUESS I'LL TALK TO KYLE.

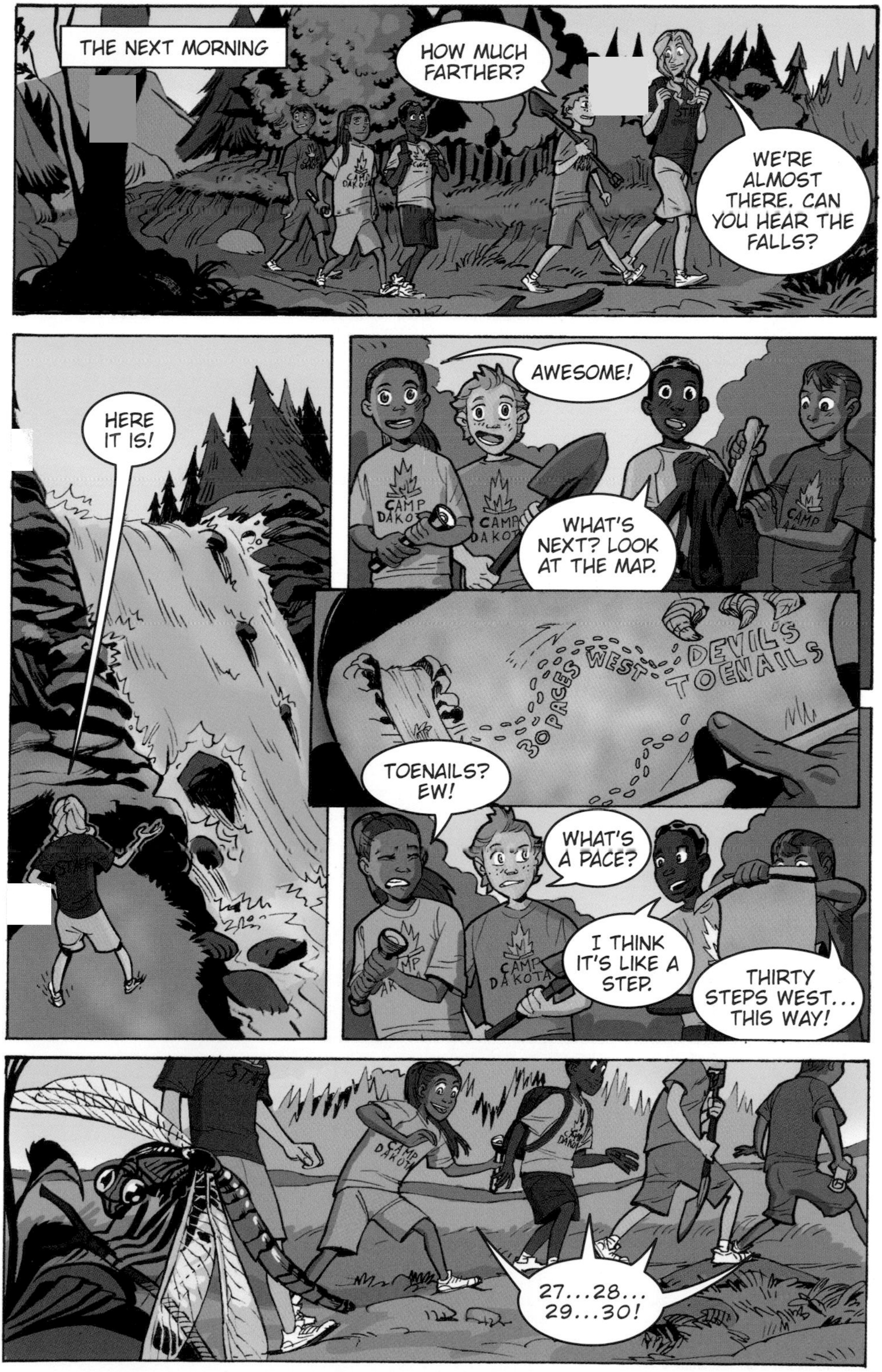
THE NEXT MORNING
HOW MUCH FARTHER?
WE'RE ALMOST THERE. CAN YOU HEAR THE FALLS?
HERE IT IS!
AWESOME!
WHAT'S NEXT? LOOK AT THE MAP.
30 PACES WEST
DEVIL'S TOENAILS
TOENAILS? EW!
WHAT'S A PACE?
I THINK IT'S LIKE A STEP.
THIRTY STEPS WEST... THIS WAY!
27...28... 29...30!

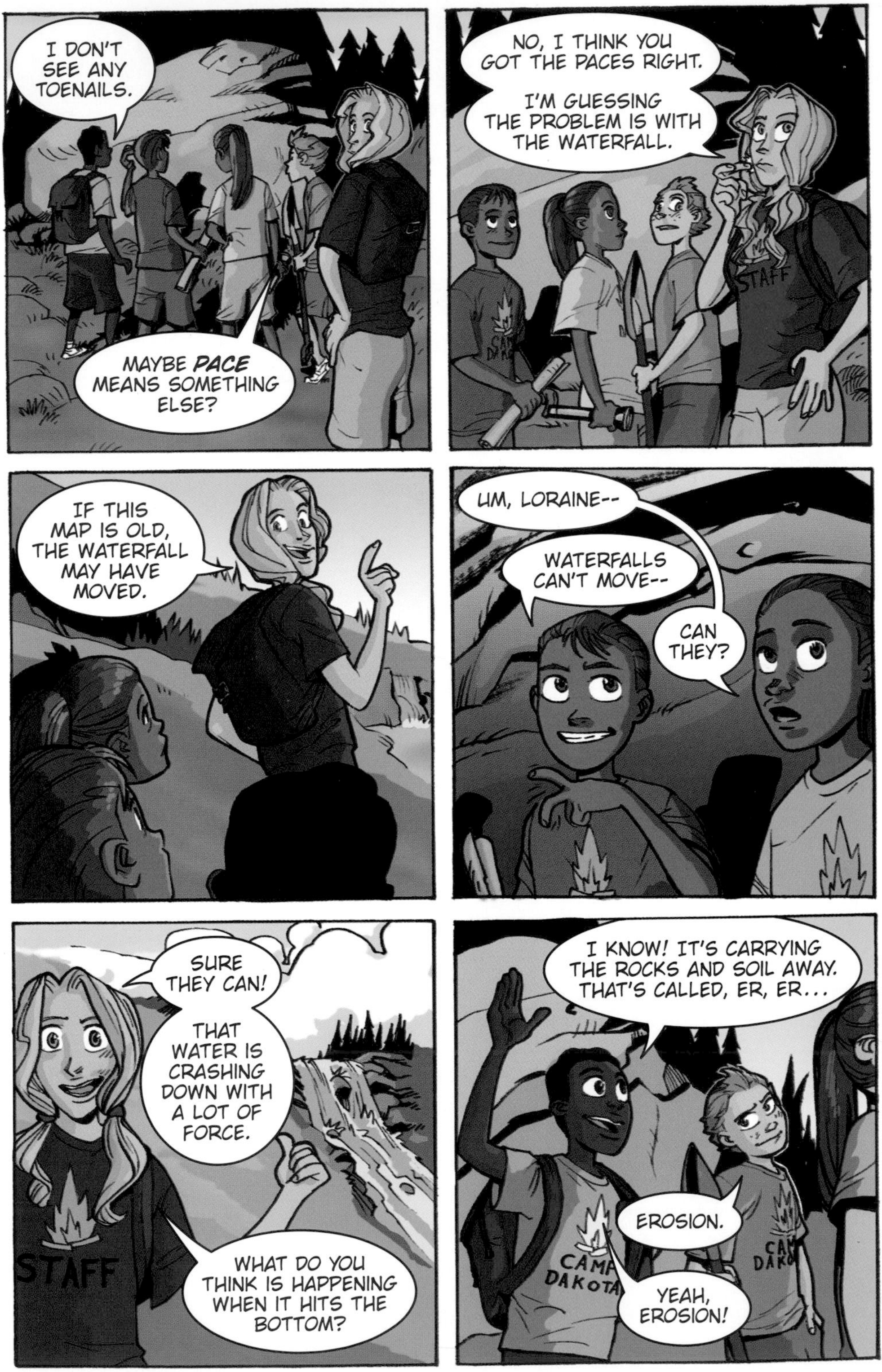

I DON'T SEE ANY TOENAILS.
MAYBE *PACE* MEANS SOMETHING ELSE?
NO, I THINK YOU GOT THE PACES RIGHT.
I'M GUESSING THE PROBLEM IS WITH THE WATERFALL.
STAFF
CAMP DAKO
IF THIS MAP IS OLD, THE WATERFALL MAY HAVE MOVED.
UM, LORAINE--
WATERFALLS CAN'T MOVE--
CAN THEY?
SURE THEY CAN!
THAT WATER IS CRASHING DOWN WITH A LOT OF FORCE.
STAFF
WHAT DO YOU THINK IS HAPPENING WHEN IT HITS THE BOTTOM?
I KNOW! IT'S CARRYING THE ROCKS AND SOIL AWAY. THAT'S CALLED, ER, ER...
CAMP DAKOTA
CAMP DAKO
EROSION.
YEAH, EROSION!

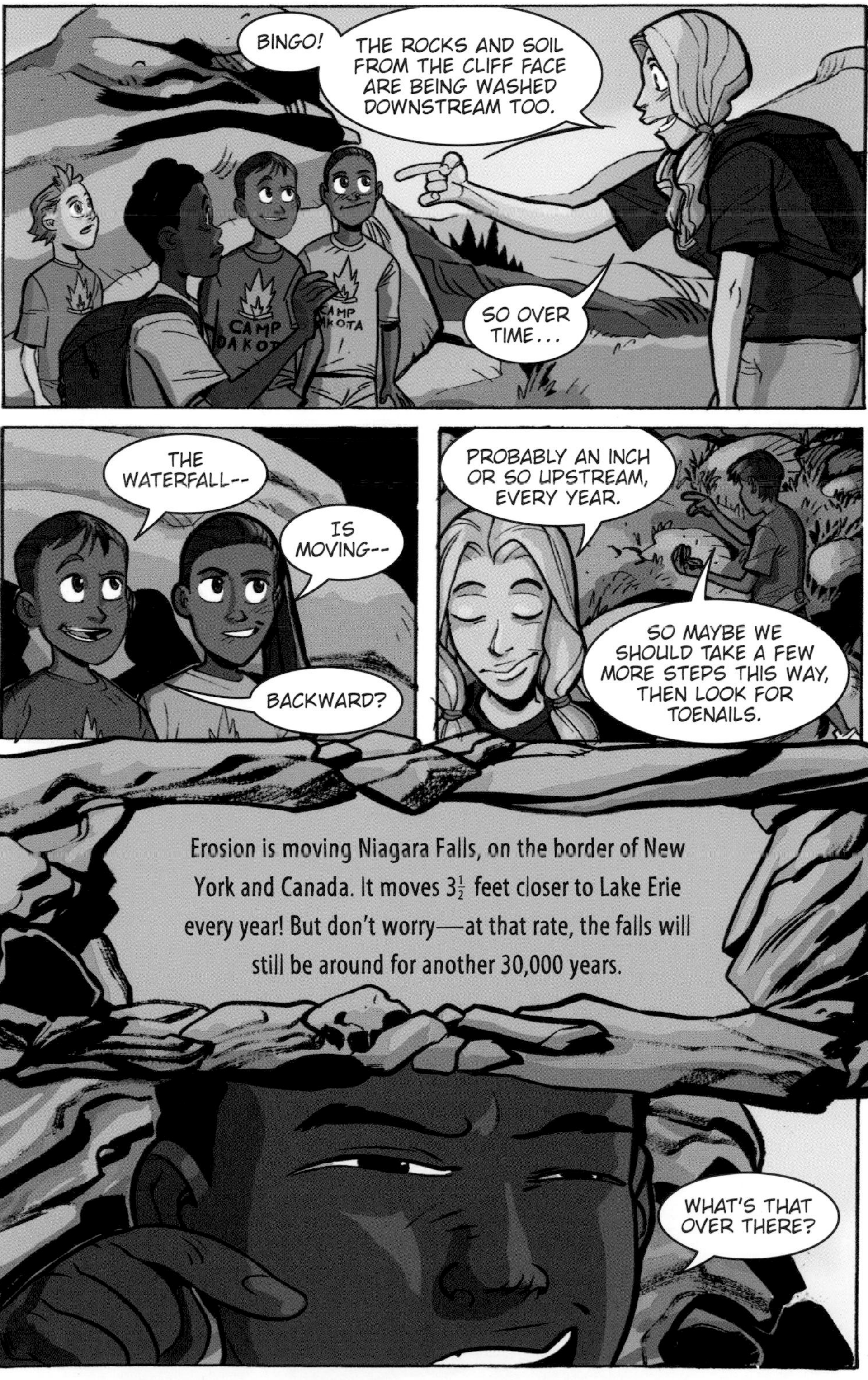
BINGO!
THE ROCKS AND SOIL FROM THE CLIFF FACE ARE BEING WASHED DOWNSTREAM TOO.
CAMP DAKOTA
CAMP DAKOTA
SO OVER TIME...
THE WATERFALL--
IS MOVING--
BACKWARD?
PROBABLY AN INCH OR SO UPSTREAM, EVERY YEAR.
SO MAYBE WE SHOULD TAKE A FEW MORE STEPS THIS WAY, THEN LOOK FOR TOENAILS.
Erosion is moving Niagara Falls, on the border of New York and Canada. It moves $3\frac{1}{2}$ feet closer to Lake Erie every year! But don't worry—at that rate, the falls will still be around for another 30,000 years.
WHAT'S THAT OVER THERE?

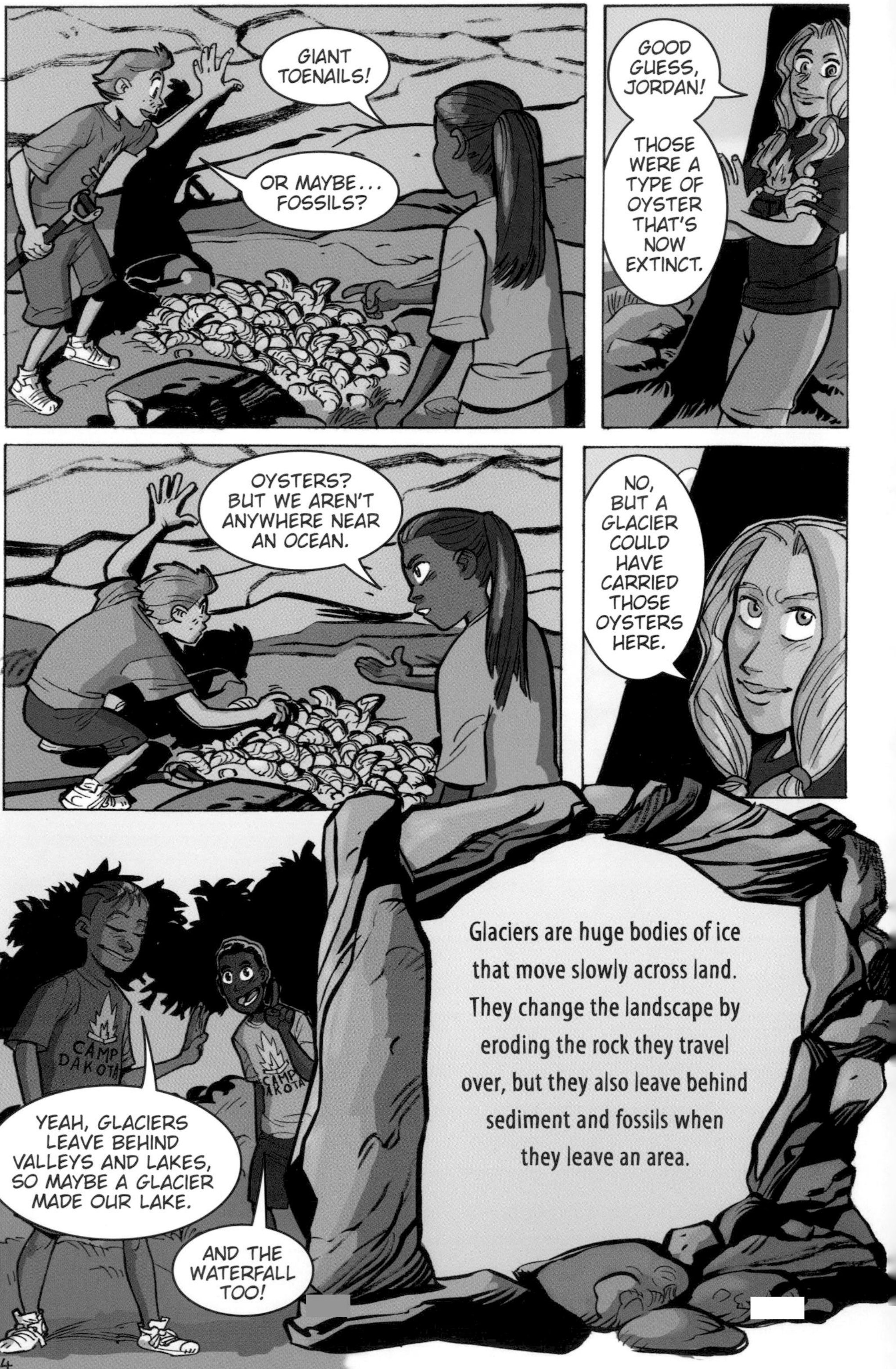
GIANT TOENAILS!
OR MAYBE... FOSSILS?
GOOD GUESS, JORDAN!
THOSE WERE A TYPE OF OYSTER THAT'S NOW EXTINCT.
OYSTERS? BUT WE AREN'T ANYWHERE NEAR AN OCEAN.
NO, BUT A GLACIER COULD HAVE CARRIED THOSE OYSTERS HERE.
Glaciers are huge bodies of ice that move slowly across land. They change the landscape by eroding the rock they travel over, but they also leave behind sediment and fossils when they leave an area.
CAMP DAKOTA
CAMP DAKOTA
YEAH, GLACIERS LEAVE BEHIND VALLEYS AND LAKES, SO MAYBE A GLACIER MADE OUR LAKE.
AND THE WATERFALL TOO!

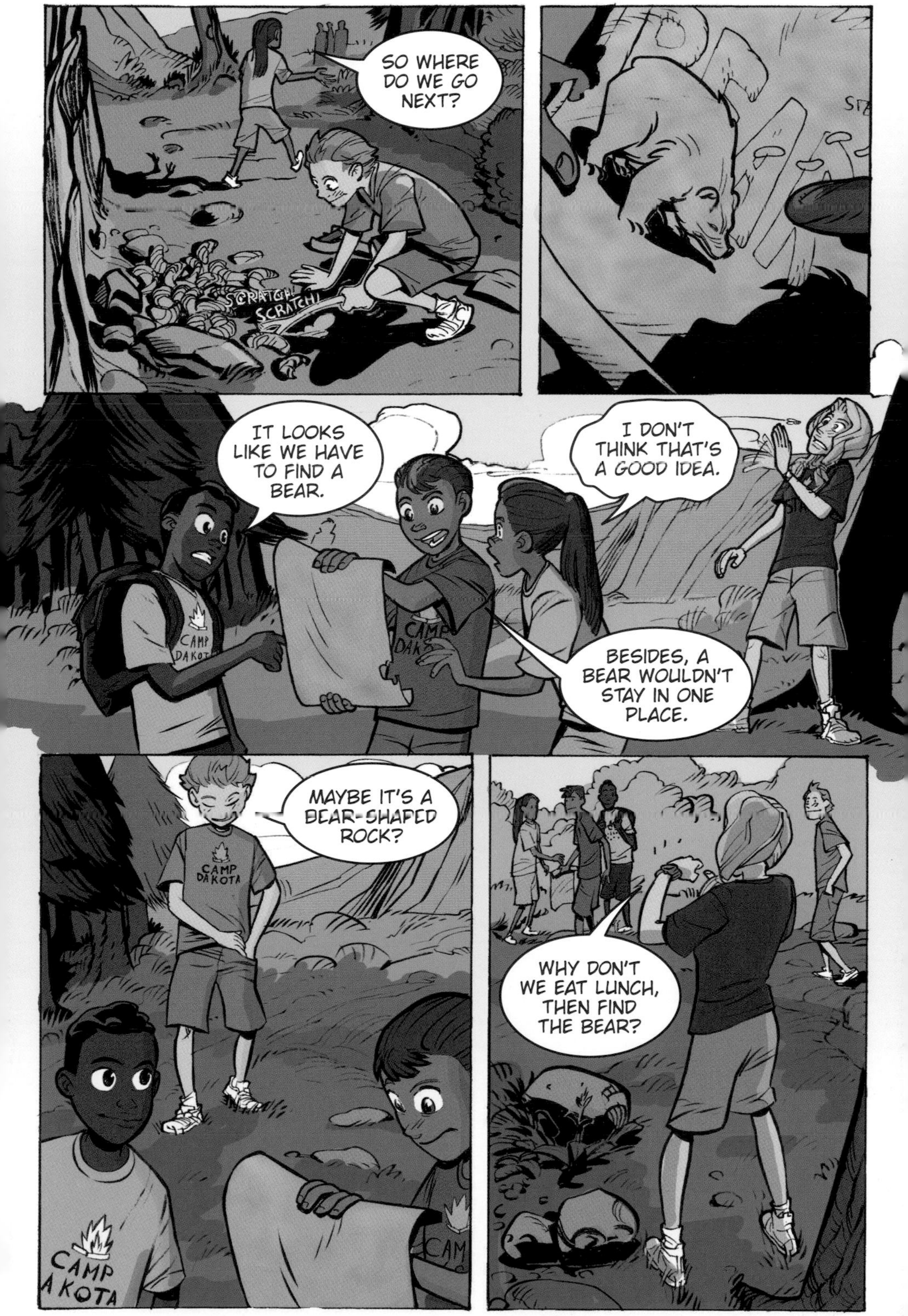
SO WHERE DO WE GO NEXT?
SCRATCH! SCRATCH!
IT LOOKS LIKE WE HAVE TO FIND A BEAR.
I DON'T THINK THAT'S A GOOD IDEA.
BESIDES, A BEAR WOULDN'T STAY IN ONE PLACE.
MAYBE IT'S A BEAR-SHAPED ROCK?
WHY DON'T WE EAT LUNCH, THEN FIND THE BEAR?

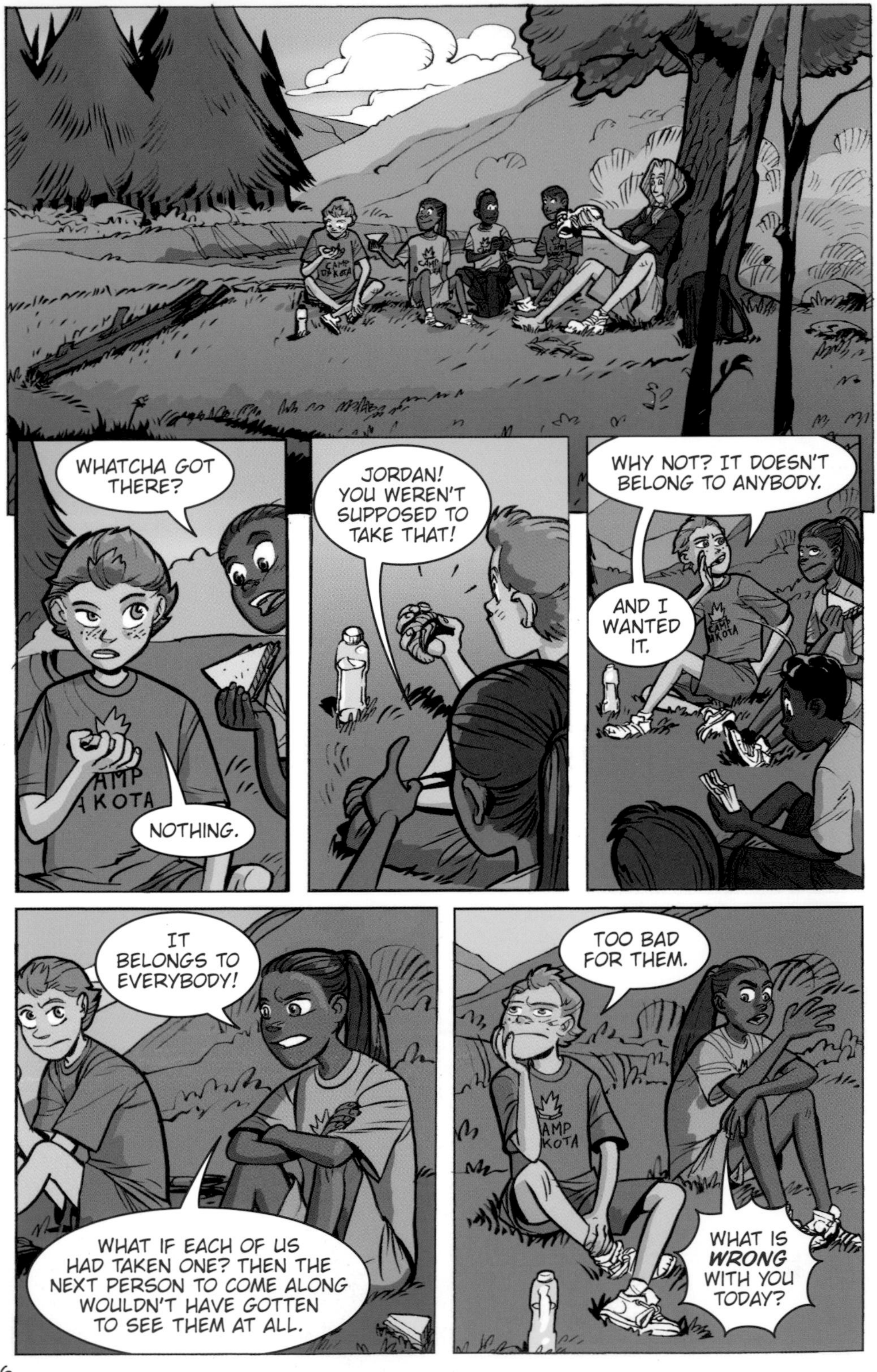
WHATCHA GOT THERE?
NOTHING.
JORDAN! YOU WEREN'T SUPPOSED TO TAKE THAT!
WHY NOT? IT DOESN'T BELONG TO ANYBODY.
AND I WANTED IT.
IT BELONGS TO EVERYBODY!
WHAT IF EACH OF US HAD TAKEN ONE? THEN THE NEXT PERSON TO COME ALONG WOULDN'T HAVE GOTTEN TO SEE THEM AT ALL.
TOO BAD FOR THEM.
WHAT IS *WRONG* WITH YOU TODAY?

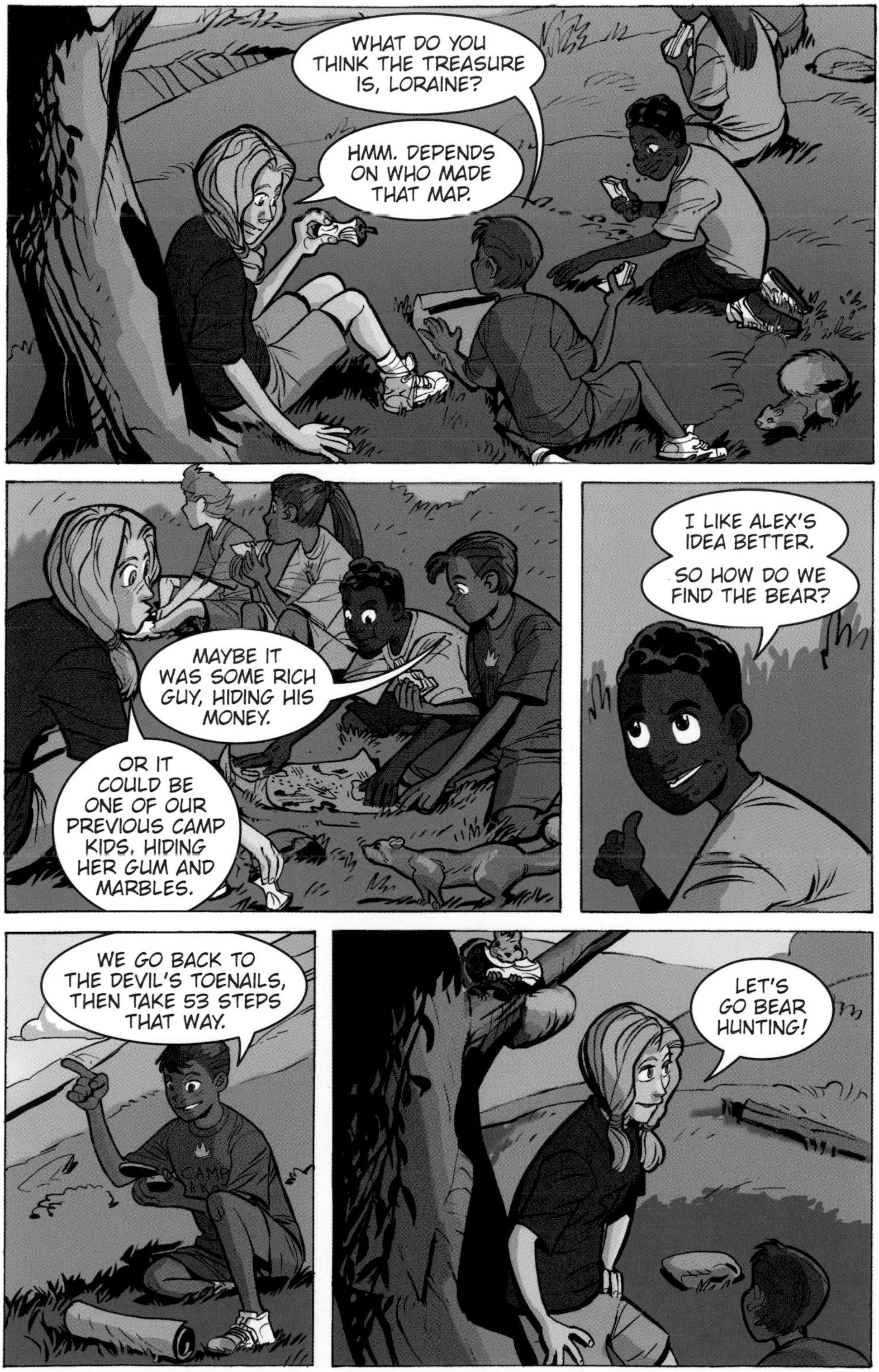
WHAT DO YOU THINK THE TREASURE IS, LORAINE?
HMM. DEPENDS ON WHO MADE THAT MAP.
MAYBE IT WAS SOME RICH GUY, HIDING HIS MONEY.
OR IT COULD BE ONE OF OUR PREVIOUS CAMP KIDS, HIDING HER GUM AND MARBLES.
I LIKE ALEX'S IDEA BETTER.
SO HOW DO WE FIND THE BEAR?
WE GO BACK TO THE DEVIL'S TOENAILS, THEN TAKE 53 STEPS THAT WAY.
LET'S GO BEAR HUNTING!

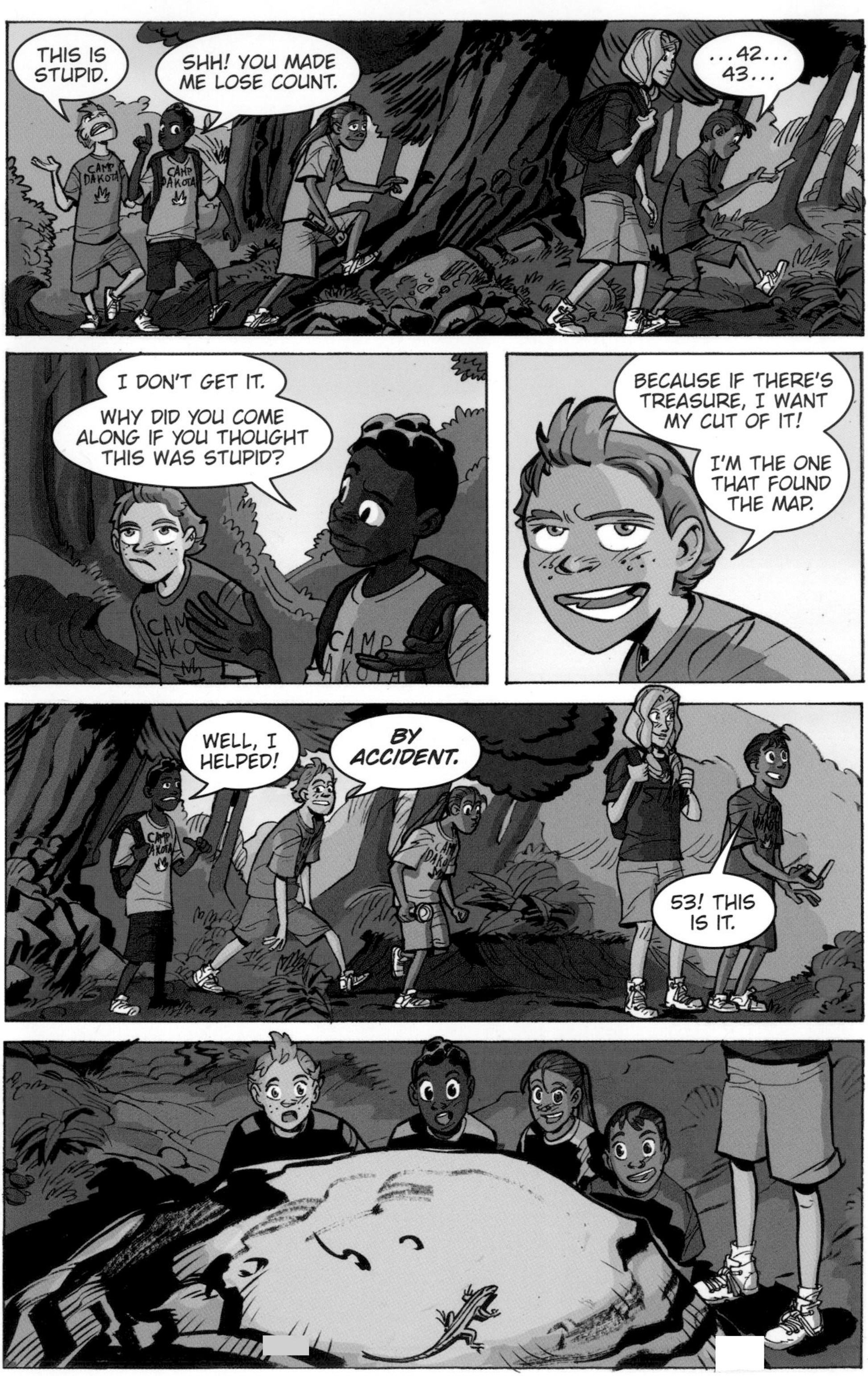
THIS IS STUPID.
SHH! YOU MADE ME LOSE COUNT.
...42... 43...
I DON'T GET IT.
WHY DID YOU COME ALONG IF YOU THOUGHT THIS WAS STUPID?
BECAUSE IF THERE'S TREASURE, I WANT MY CUT OF IT!
I'M THE ONE THAT FOUND THE MAP.
WELL, I HELPED!
BY ACCIDENT.
53! THIS IS IT.

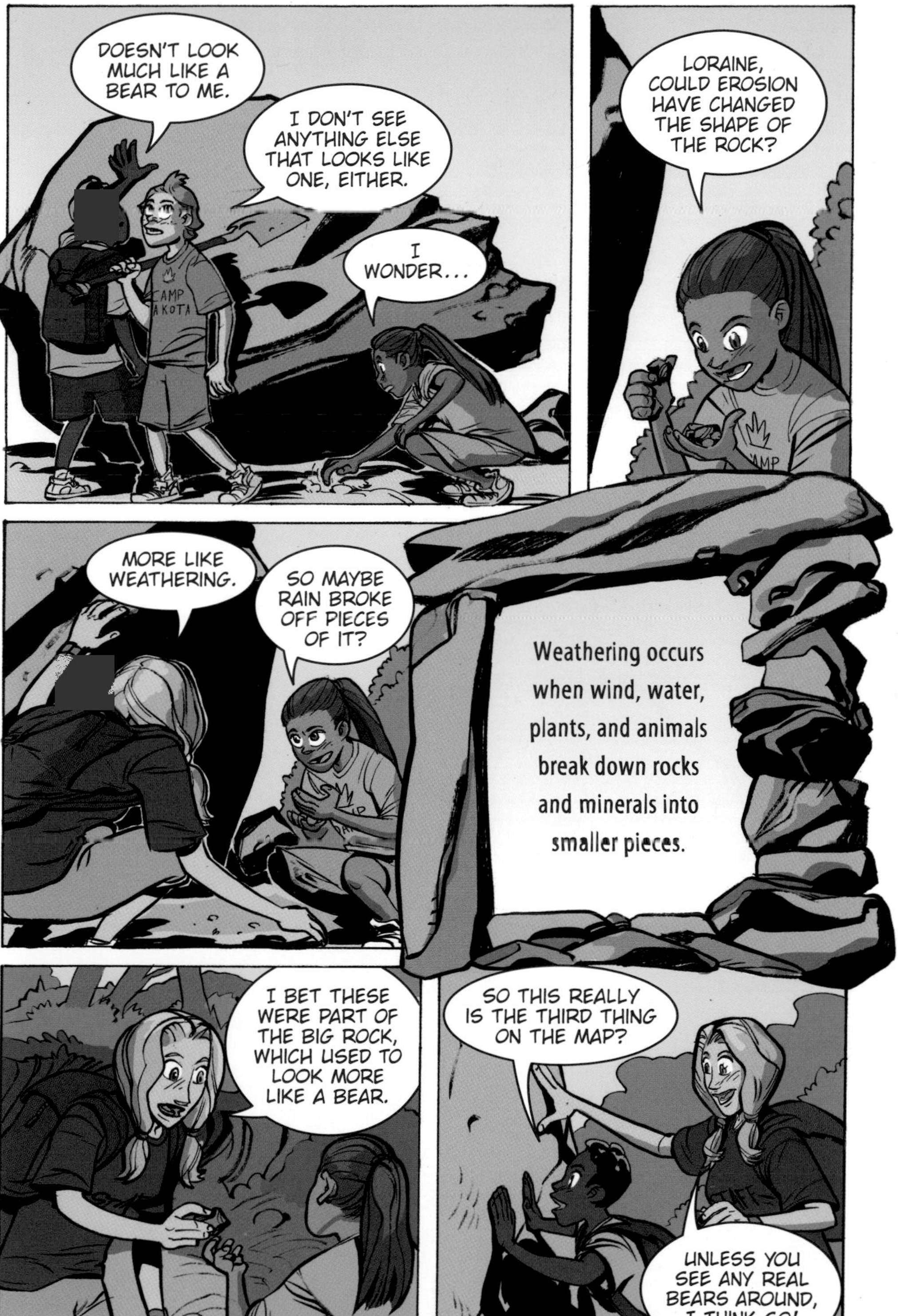
DOESN'T LOOK MUCH LIKE A BEAR TO ME.
I DON'T SEE ANYTHING ELSE THAT LOOKS LIKE ONE, EITHER.
I WONDER...
CAMP DAKOTA
LORAINE, COULD EROSION HAVE CHANGED THE SHAPE OF THE ROCK?
MORE LIKE WEATHERING.
SO MAYBE RAIN BROKE OFF PIECES OF IT?
Weathering occurs when wind, water, plants, and animals break down rocks and minerals into smaller pieces.
I BET THESE WERE PART OF THE BIG ROCK, WHICH USED TO LOOK MORE LIKE A BEAR.
SO THIS REALLY IS THE THIRD THING ON THE MAP?
UNLESS YOU SEE ANY REAL BEARS AROUND, I THINK SO!

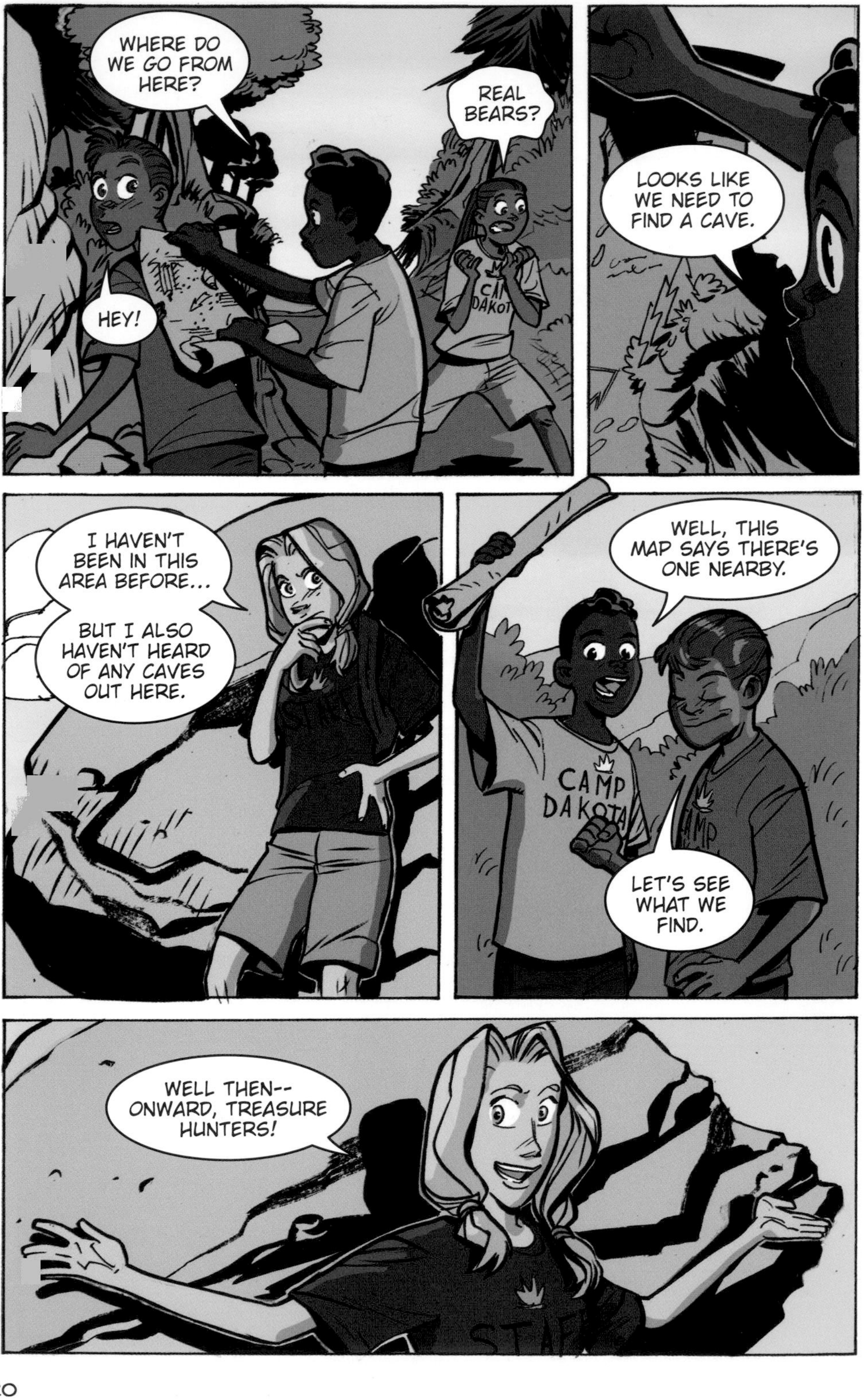
WHERE DO WE GO FROM HERE?
HEY!
REAL BEARS?
CAMP DAKOTA
LOOKS LIKE WE NEED TO FIND A CAVE.
I HAVEN'T BEEN IN THIS AREA BEFORE...
BUT I ALSO HAVEN'T HEARD OF ANY CAVES OUT HERE.
WELL, THIS MAP SAYS THERE'S ONE NEARBY.
CAMP DAKOTA
LET'S SEE WHAT WE FIND.
WELL THEN-- ONWARD, TREASURE HUNTERS!

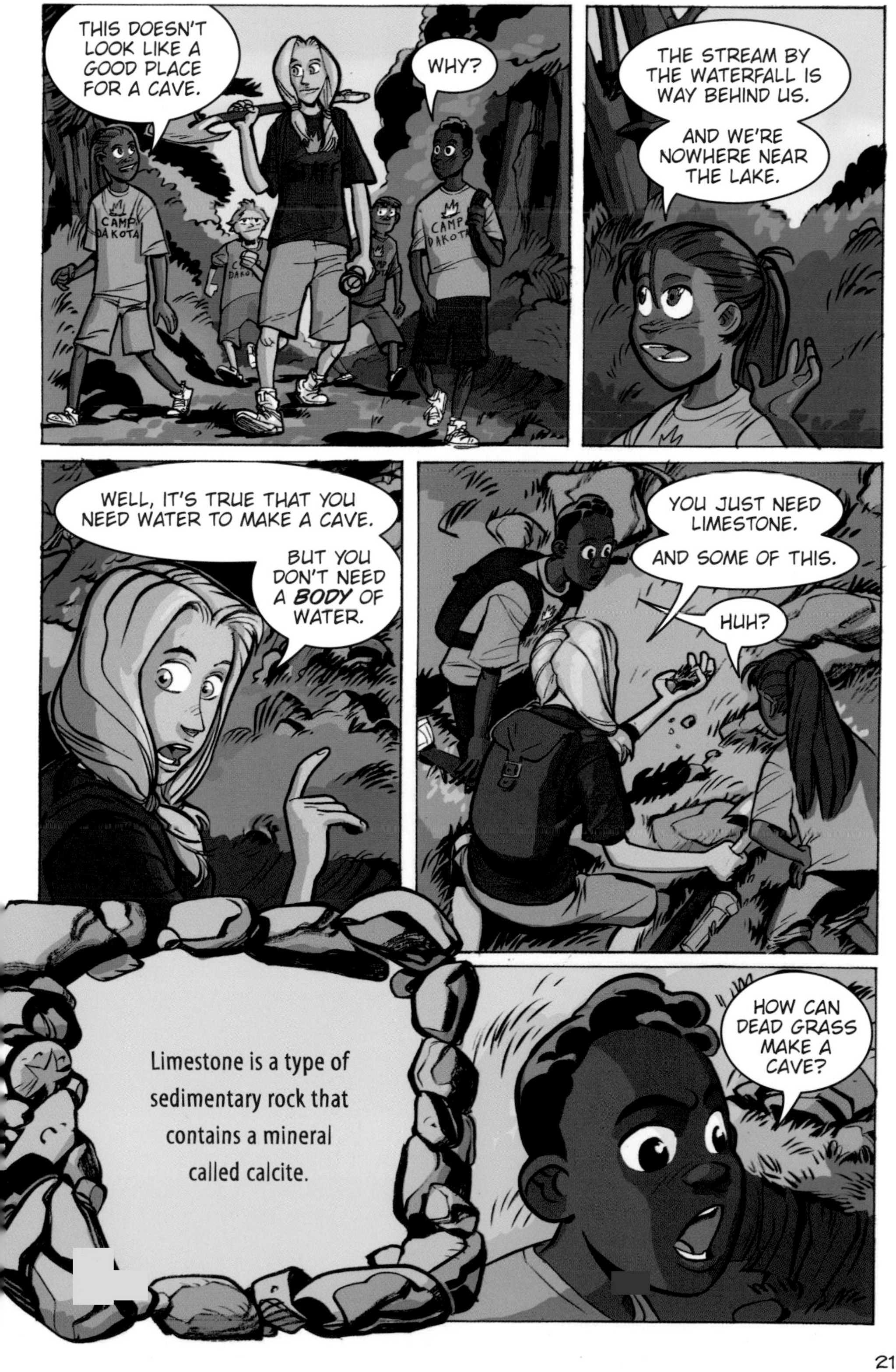
THIS DOESN'T LOOK LIKE A GOOD PLACE FOR A CAVE.
WHY?
THE STREAM BY THE WATERFALL IS WAY BEHIND US.
AND WE'RE NOWHERE NEAR THE LAKE.
WELL, IT'S TRUE THAT YOU NEED WATER TO MAKE A CAVE.
BUT YOU DON'T NEED A *BODY* OF WATER.
YOU JUST NEED LIMESTONE.
AND SOME OF THIS.
HUH?
Limestone is a type of sedimentary rock that contains a mineral called calcite.
HOW CAN DEAD GRASS MAKE A CAVE?

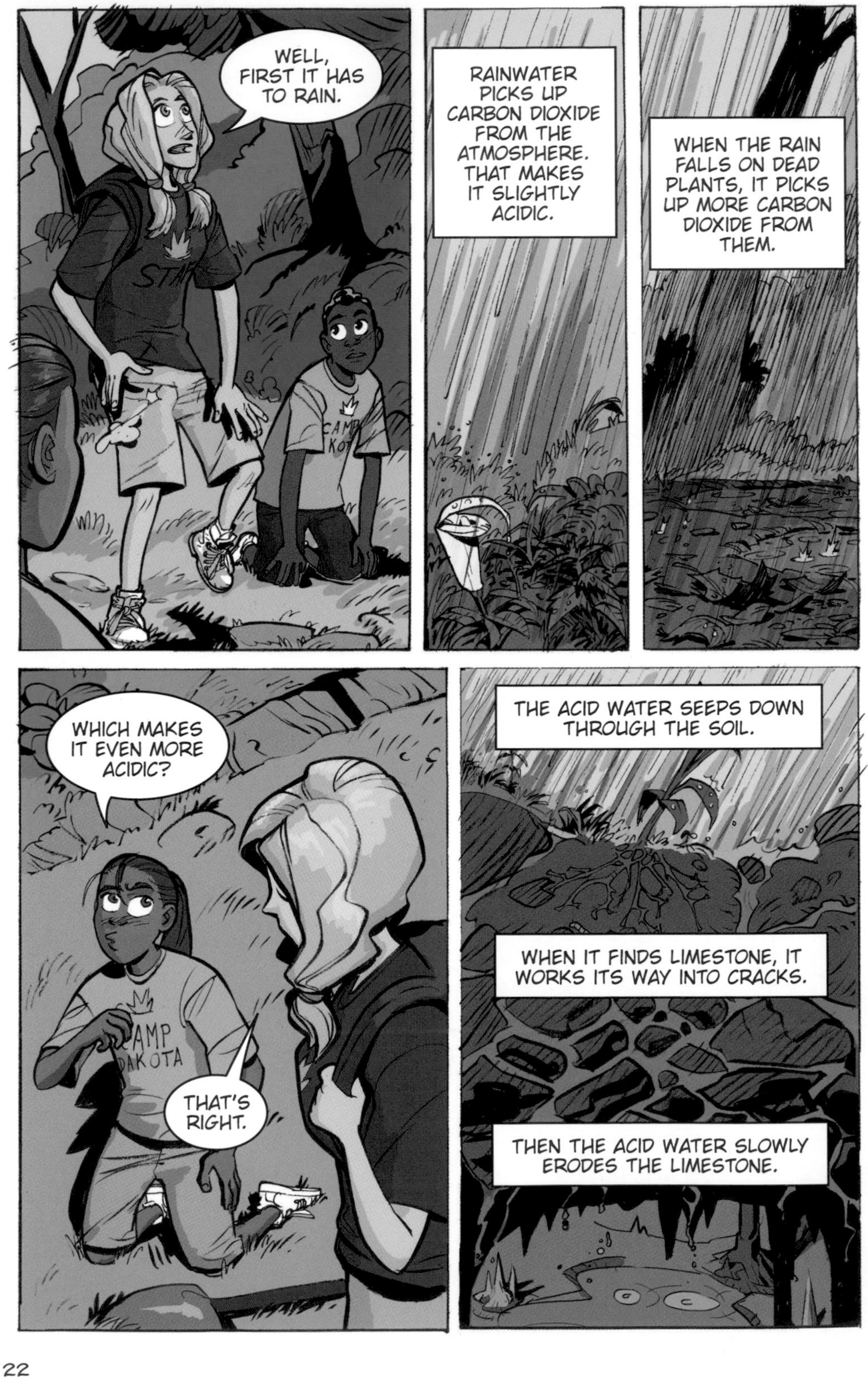
WELL, FIRST IT HAS TO RAIN.
RAINWATER PICKS UP CARBON DIOXIDE FROM THE ATMOSPHERE. THAT MAKES IT SLIGHTLY ACIDIC.
WHEN THE RAIN FALLS ON DEAD PLANTS, IT PICKS UP MORE CARBON DIOXIDE FROM THEM.
WHICH MAKES IT EVEN MORE ACIDIC?
THAT'S RIGHT.
THE ACID WATER SEEPS DOWN THROUGH THE SOIL.
WHEN IT FINDS LIMESTONE, IT WORKS ITS WAY INTO CRACKS.
THEN THE ACID WATER SLOWLY ERODES THE LIMESTONE.

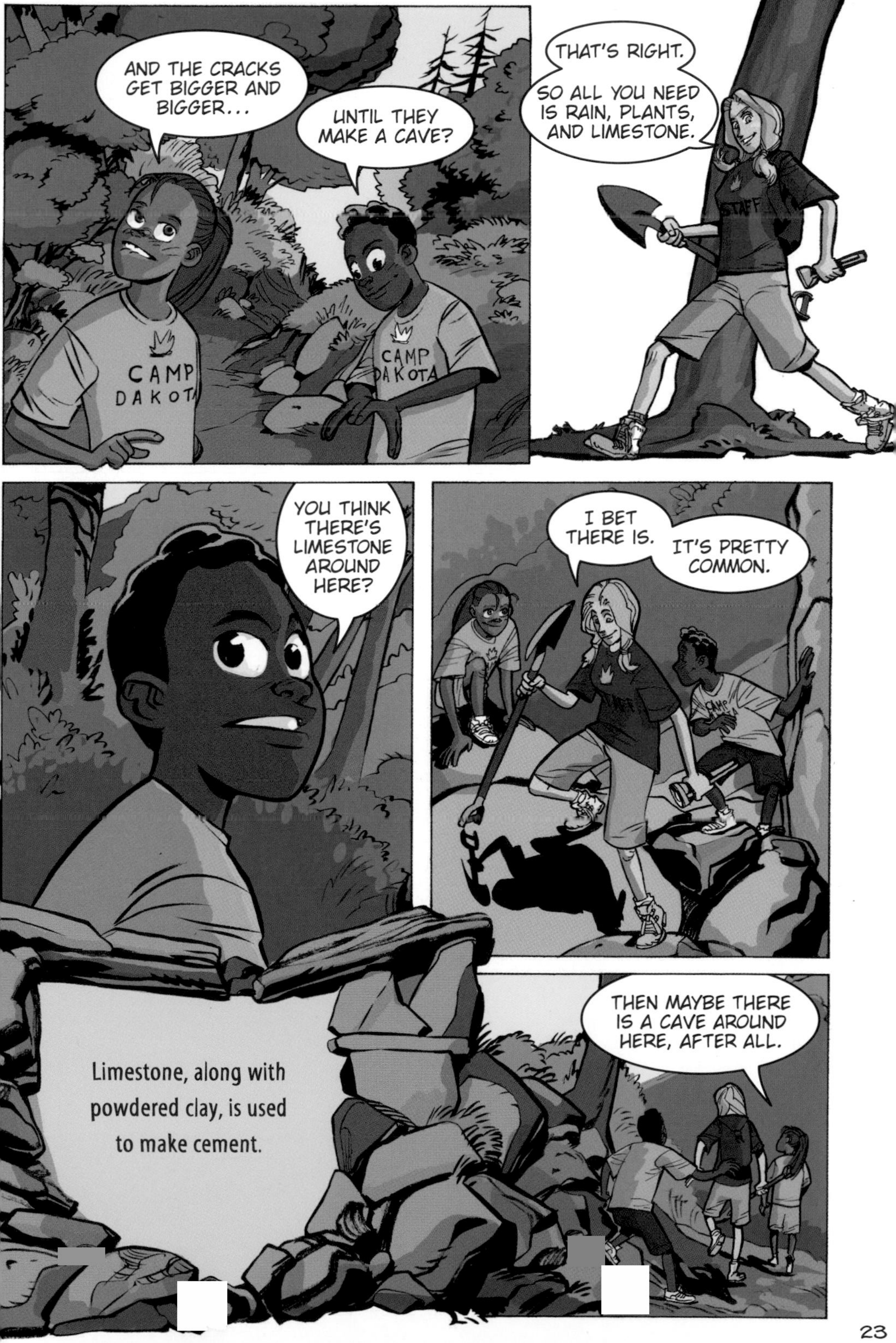
AND THE CRACKS GET BIGGER AND BIGGER...
UNTIL THEY MAKE A CAVE?
THAT'S RIGHT.
SO ALL YOU NEED IS RAIN, PLANTS, AND LIMESTONE.
CAMP DAKOTA
CAMP DAKOTA
STAFF
YOU THINK THERE'S LIMESTONE AROUND HERE?
I BET THERE IS.
IT'S PRETTY COMMON.
Limestone, along with powdered clay, is used to make cement.
THEN MAYBE THERE IS A CAVE AROUND HERE, AFTER ALL.

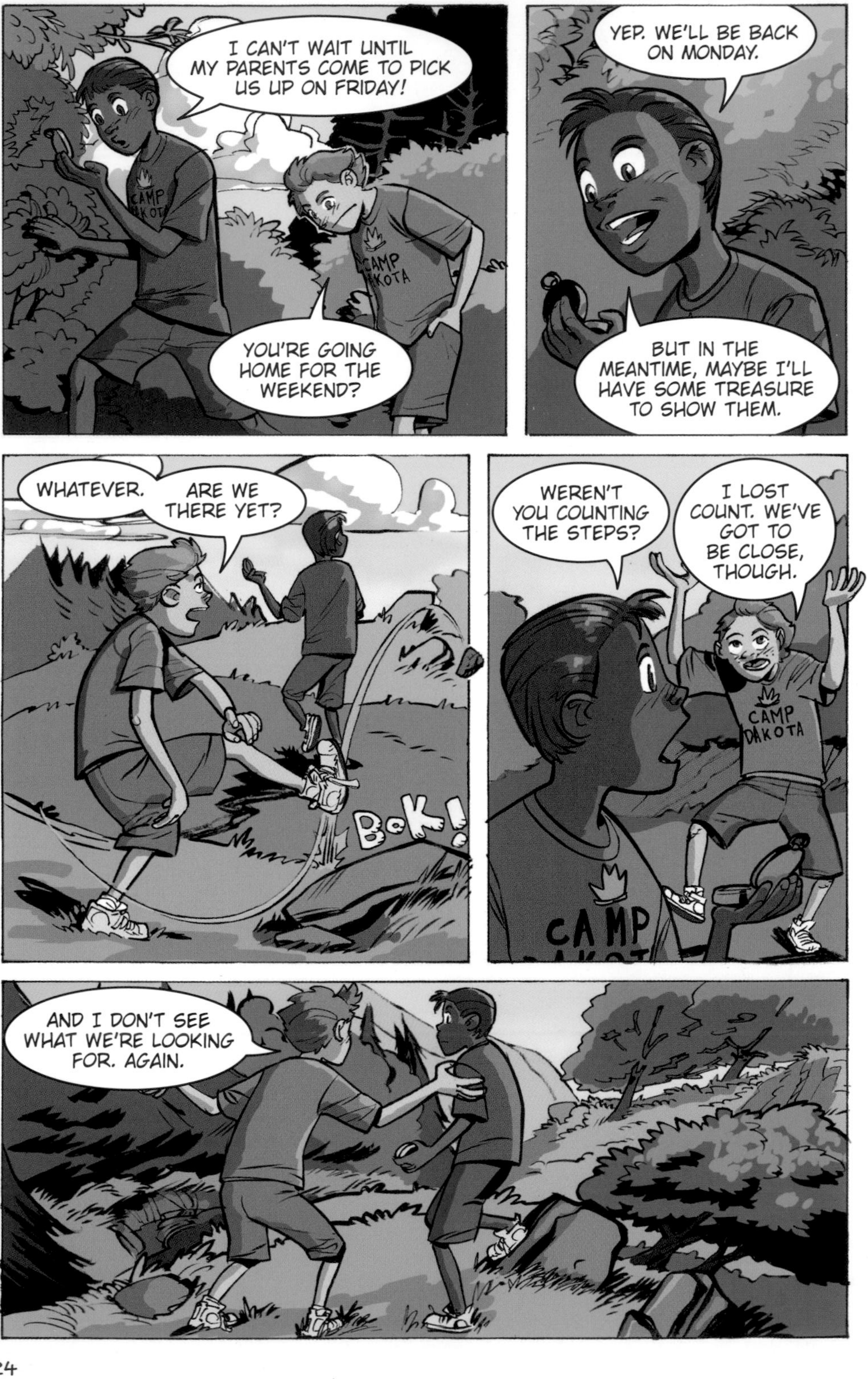
I CAN'T WAIT UNTIL MY PARENTS COME TO PICK US UP ON FRIDAY!
YOU'RE GOING HOME FOR THE WEEKEND?
YEP. WE'LL BE BACK ON MONDAY.
BUT IN THE MEANTIME, MAYBE I'LL HAVE SOME TREASURE TO SHOW THEM.
WHATEVER.
ARE WE THERE YET?
BoK!
WEREN'T YOU COUNTING THE STEPS?
I LOST COUNT. WE'VE GOT TO BE CLOSE, THOUGH.
AND I DON'T SEE WHAT WE'RE LOOKING FOR. AGAIN.

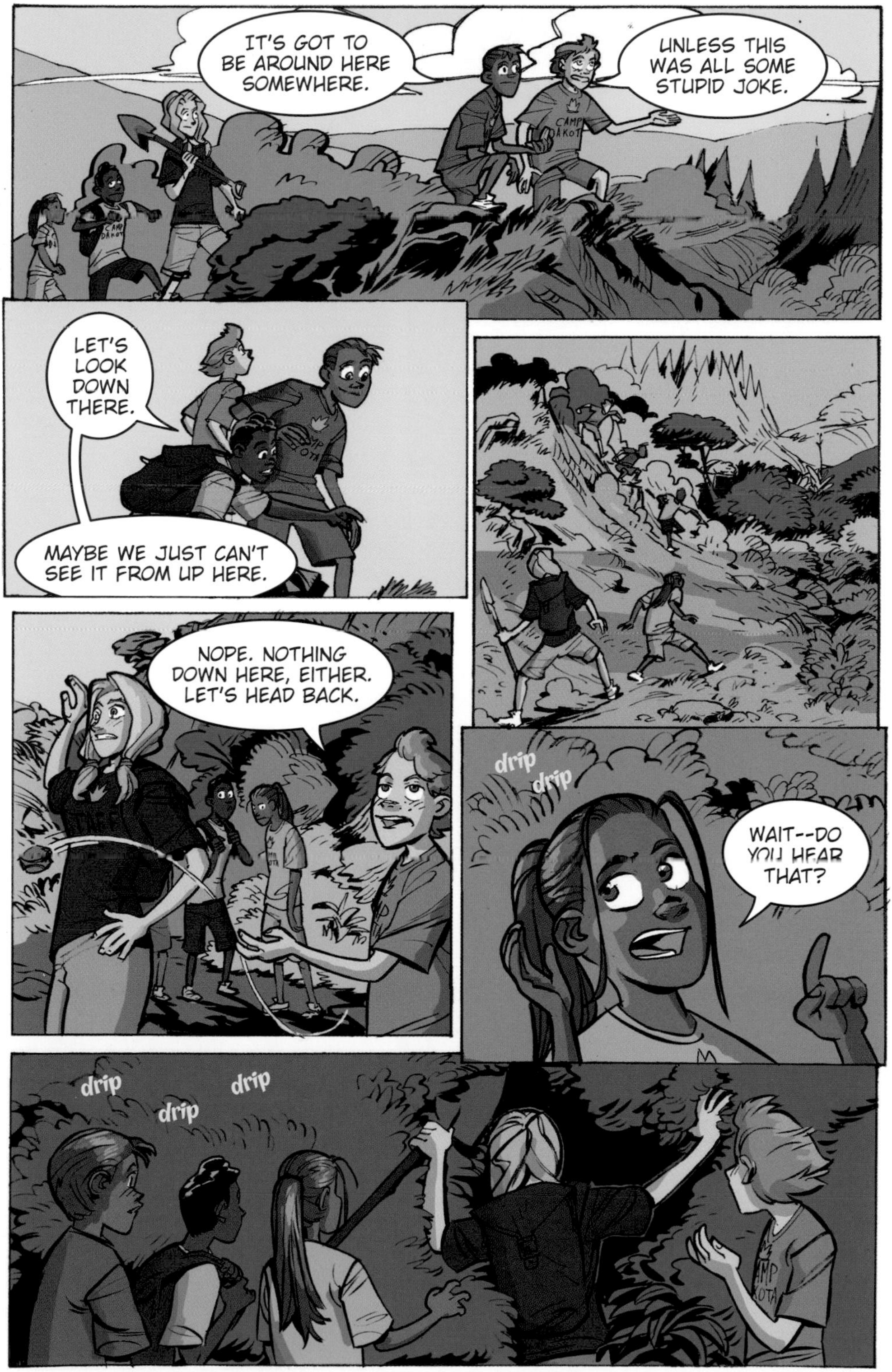
IT'S GOT TO BE AROUND HERE SOMEWHERE.
UNLESS THIS WAS ALL SOME STUPID JOKE.
CAMP DAKOTA
LET'S LOOK DOWN THERE.
MAYBE WE JUST CAN'T SEE IT FROM UP HERE.
NOPE. NOTHING DOWN HERE, EITHER. LET'S HEAD BACK.
drip
drip
WAIT--DO YOU HEAR THAT?
drip
drip
drip

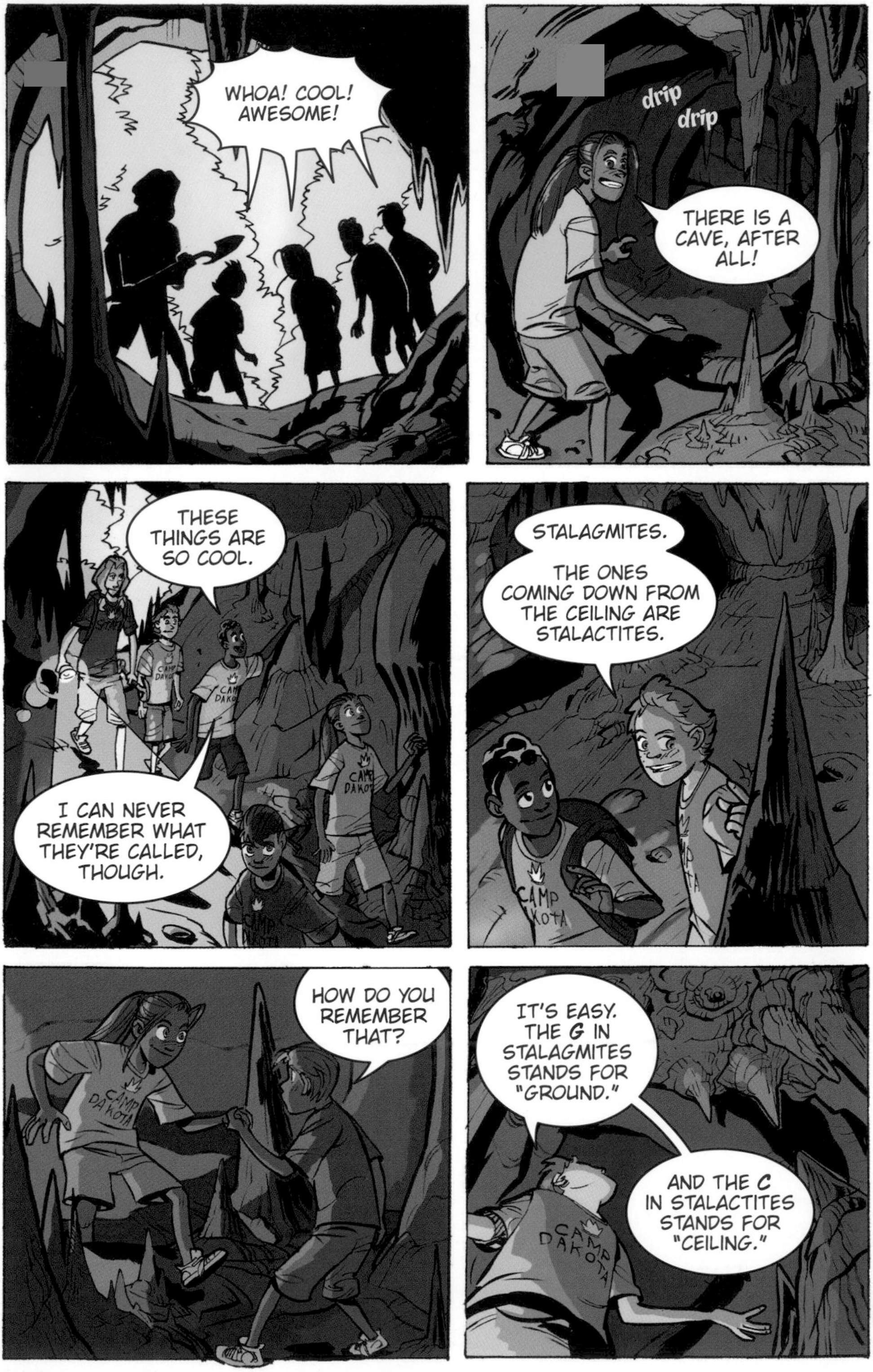
WHOA! COOL! AWESOME!
drip
drip
THERE IS A CAVE, AFTER ALL!
THESE THINGS ARE SO COOL.
I CAN NEVER REMEMBER WHAT THEY'RE CALLED, THOUGH.
STALAGMITES.
THE ONES COMING DOWN FROM THE CEILING ARE STALACTITES.
HOW DO YOU REMEMBER THAT?
IT'S EASY. THE G IN STALAGMITES STANDS FOR "GROUND."
AND THE C IN STALACTITES STANDS FOR "CEILING."

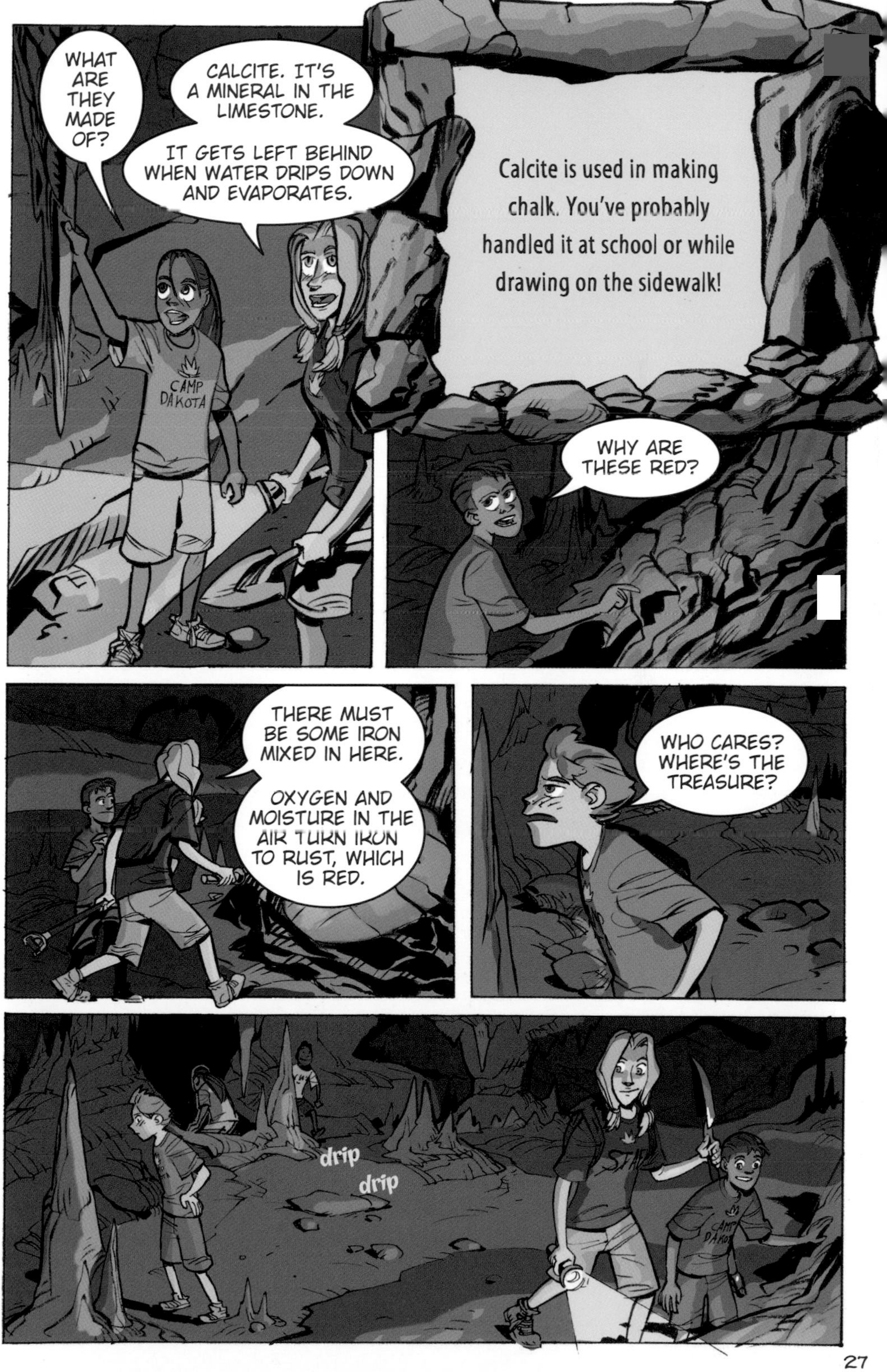
WHAT ARE THEY MADE OF?
CALCITE. IT'S A MINERAL IN THE LIMESTONE.
IT GETS LEFT BEHIND WHEN WATER DRIPS DOWN AND EVAPORATES.
Calcite is used in making chalk. You've probably handled it at school or while drawing on the sidewalk!
WHY ARE THESE RED?
THERE MUST BE SOME IRON MIXED IN HERE.
OXYGEN AND MOISTURE IN THE AIR TURN IRON TO RUST, WHICH IS RED.
WHO CARES? WHERE'S THE TREASURE?
drip
drip

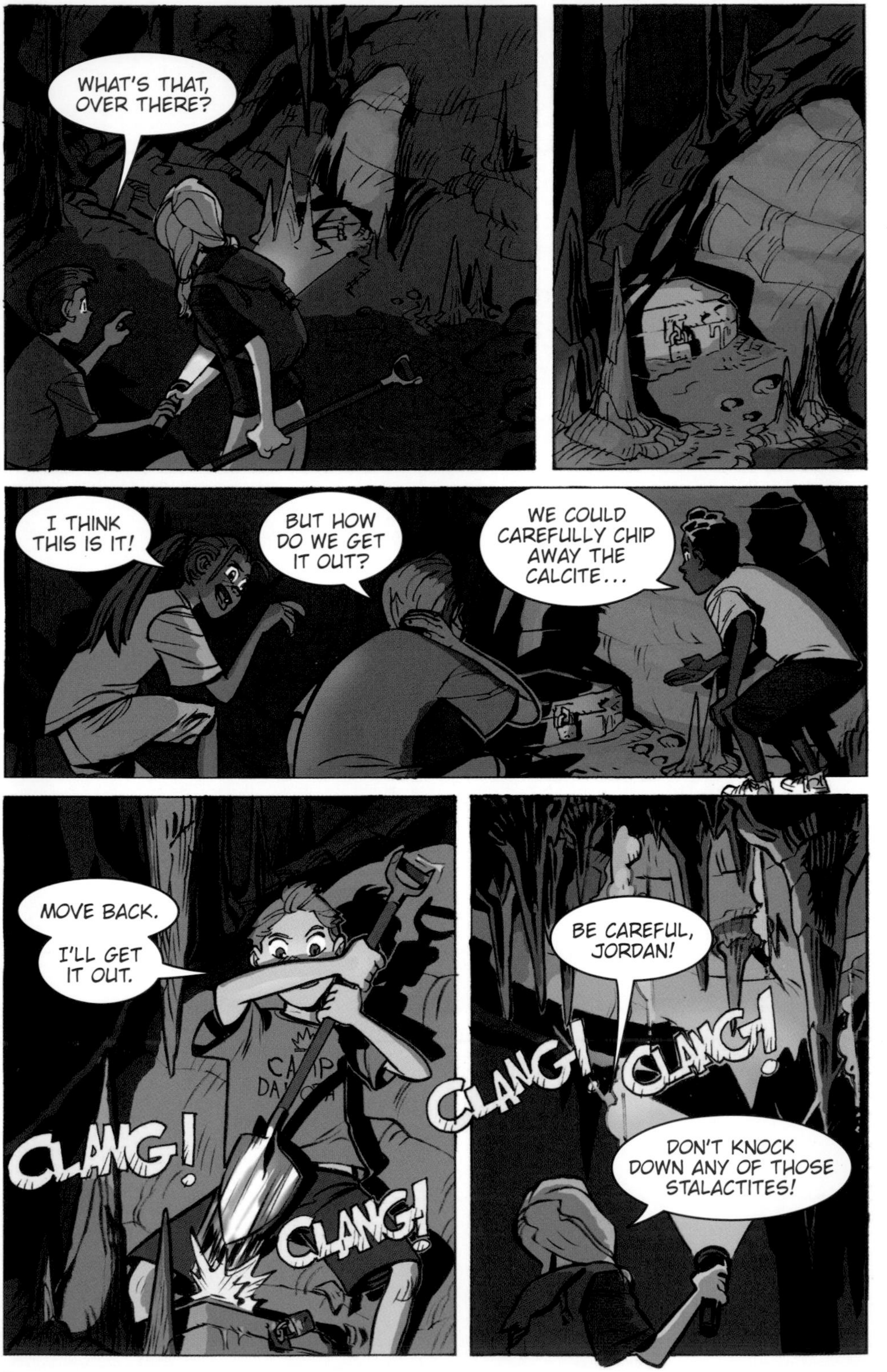
WHAT'S THAT, OVER THERE?
I THINK THIS IS IT!
BUT HOW DO WE GET IT OUT?
WE COULD CAREFULLY CHIP AWAY THE CALCITE...
MOVE BACK.
I'LL GET IT OUT.
CAMP DAKOTA
CLANG!
CLANG!
CLANG!
CLANG!
BE CAREFUL, JORDAN!
DON'T KNOCK DOWN ANY OF THOSE STALACTITES!

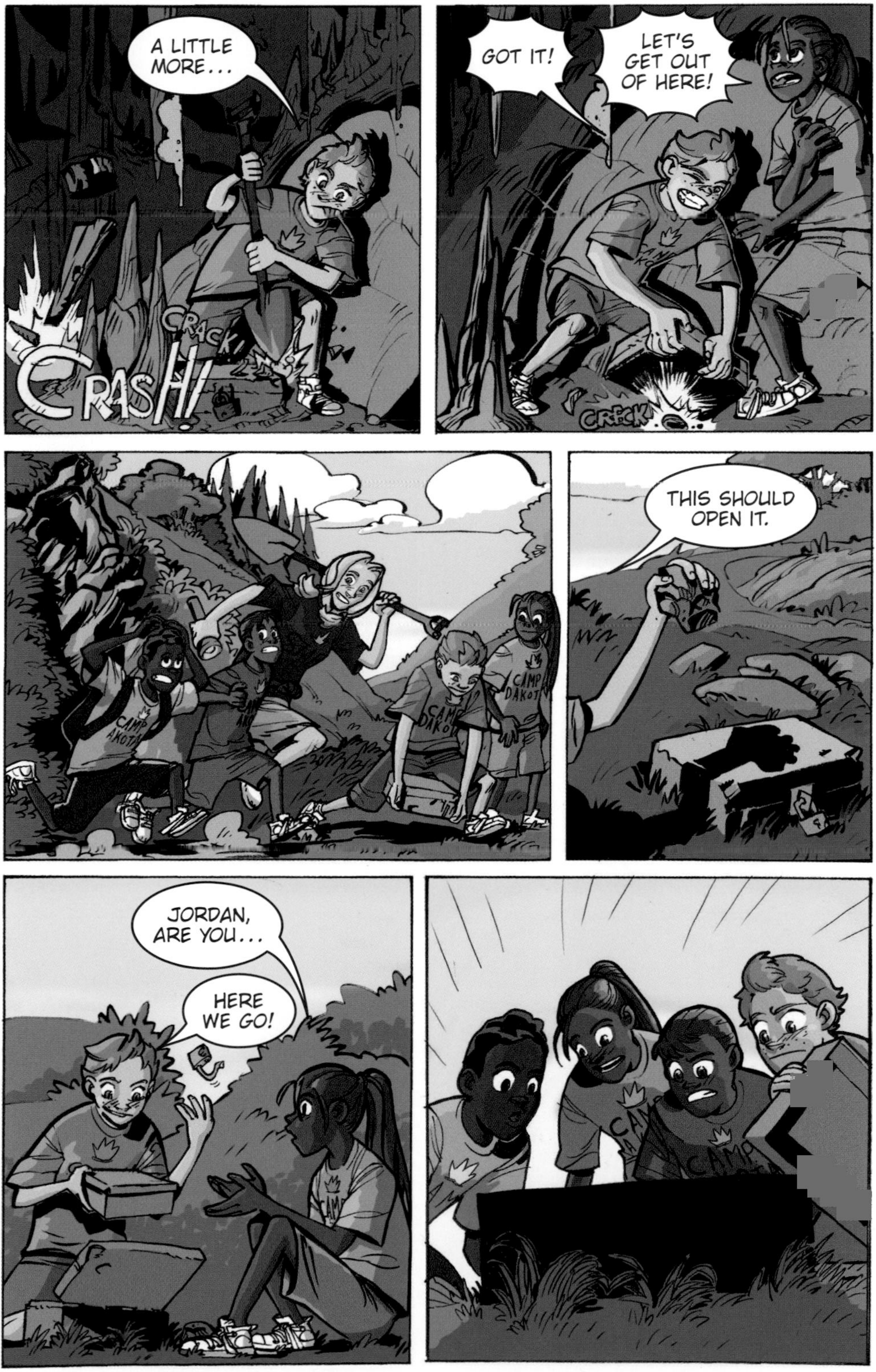
A LITTLE MORE...
CRACK!
CRASH!
GOT IT!
LET'S GET OUT OF HERE!
THIS SHOULD OPEN IT.
JORDAN, ARE YOU...
HERE WE GO!

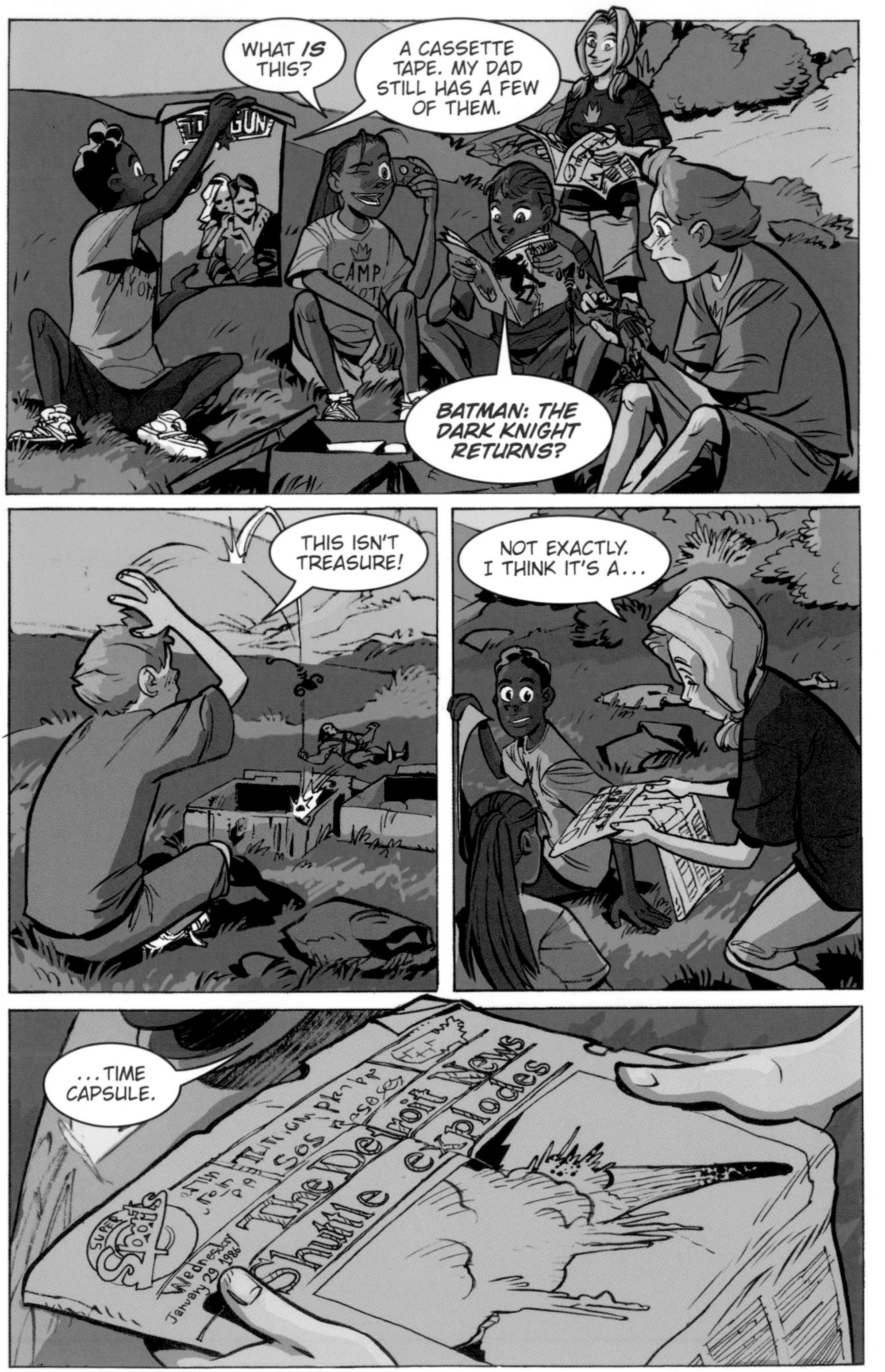
WHAT *IS* THIS?
A CASSETTE TAPE. MY DAD STILL HAS A FEW OF THEM.
*BATMAN: THE DARK KNIGHT RETURNS?*
THIS ISN'T TREASURE!
NOT EXACTLY. I THINK IT'S A...
...TIME CAPSULE.
The Detroit News
Shuttle explodes
Wednesday January 29 1986

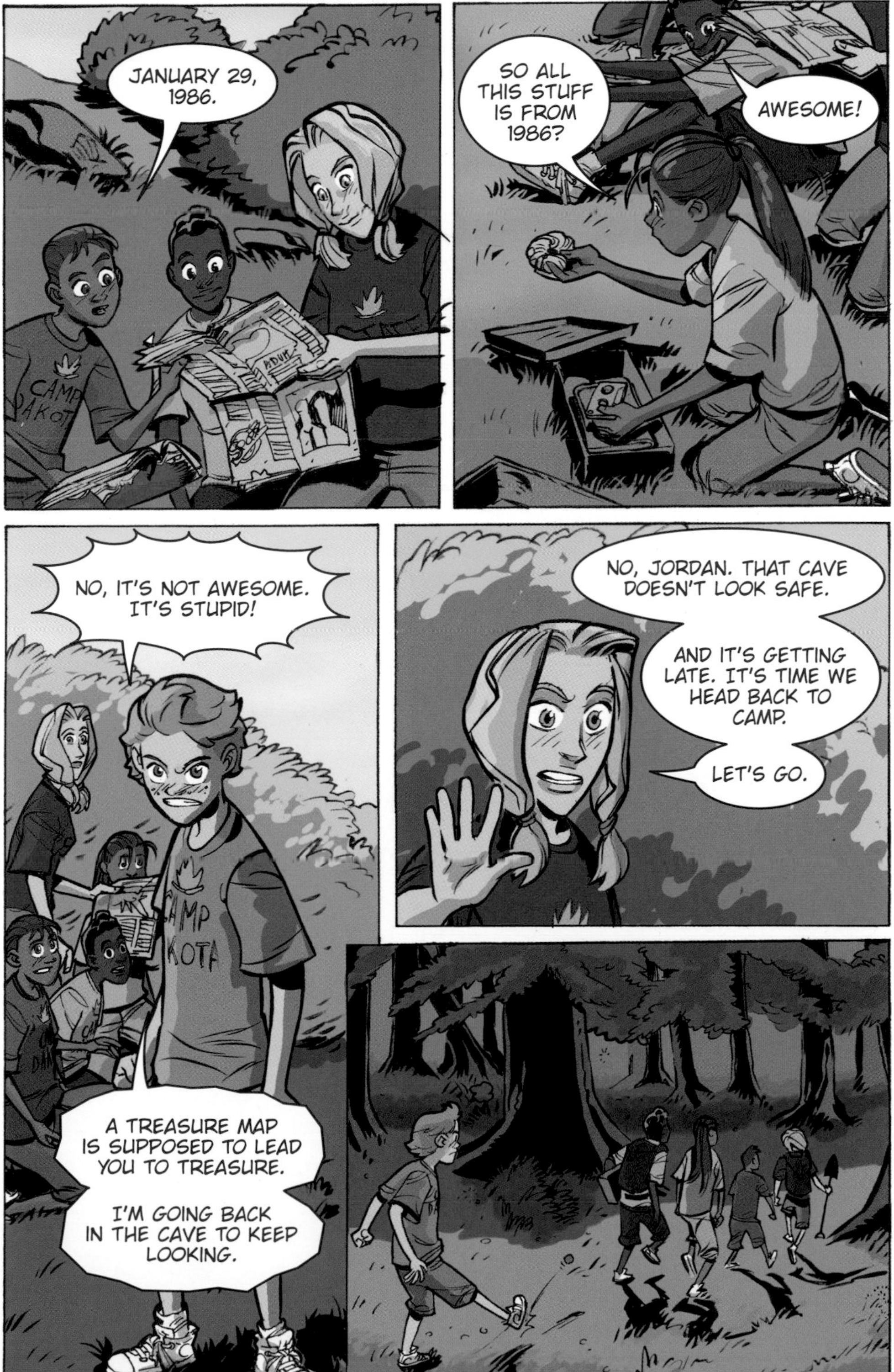
JANUARY 29, 1986.
SO ALL THIS STUFF IS FROM 1986?
AWESOME!
NO, IT'S NOT AWESOME. IT'S STUPID!
A TREASURE MAP IS SUPPOSED TO LEAD YOU TO TREASURE.
I'M GOING BACK IN THE CAVE TO KEEP LOOKING.
NO, JORDAN. THAT CAVE DOESN'T LOOK SAFE.
AND IT'S GETTING LATE. IT'S TIME WE HEAD BACK TO CAMP.
LET'S GO.

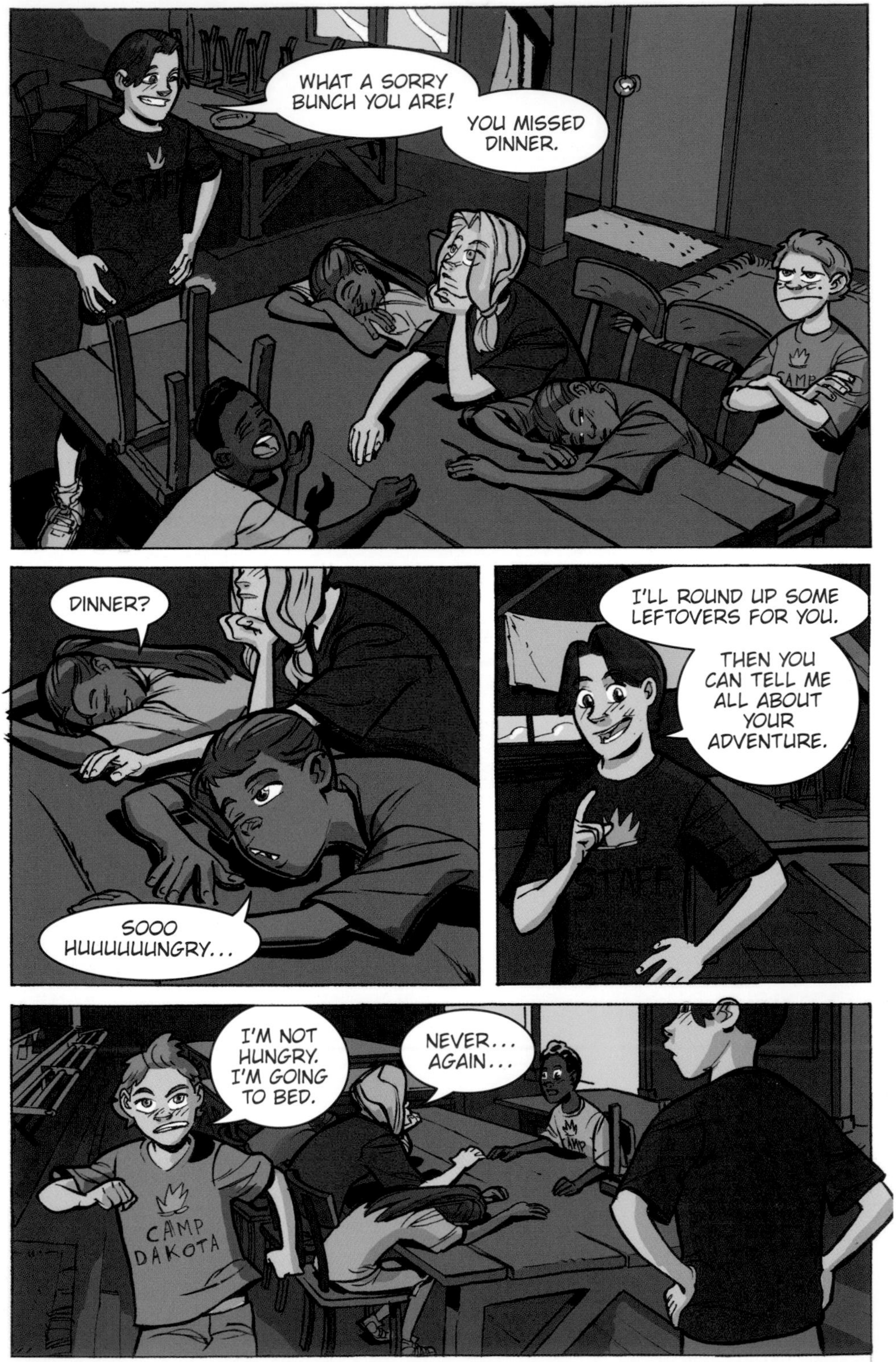
WHAT A SORRY BUNCH YOU ARE!
YOU MISSED DINNER.
STAFF
DINNER?
SOOO HUUUUUUNGRY...
I'LL ROUND UP SOME LEFTOVERS FOR YOU.
THEN YOU CAN TELL ME ALL ABOUT YOUR ADVENTURE.
STAFF
I'M NOT HUNGRY. I'M GOING TO BED.
NEVER... AGAIN...
CAMP DAKOTA

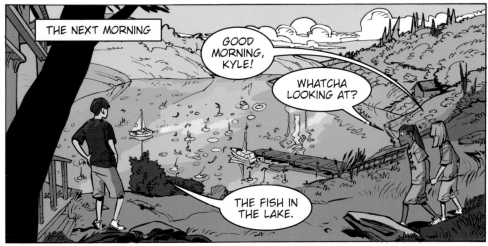

THE NEXT MORNING

GOOD MORNING, KYLE!

WHATCHA LOOKING AT?

THE FISH IN THE LAKE.

THEY'RE JUMPING AROUND.

I'VE NEVER SEEN THEM ALL DO THAT BEFORE.

MAYBE THEY'RE JUST HAPPY BECAUSE IT'S A SUNNY DAY.

THAT MUST BE IT.

LET'S GO IN AND GET SOME BREAKFAST.

MORNING, CARLY. MORNING, ANGIE.

I'M STARVING.

AFTER ALL THE LEFTOVERS YOU ATE LAST NIGHT?

I'M A GROWING BOY.

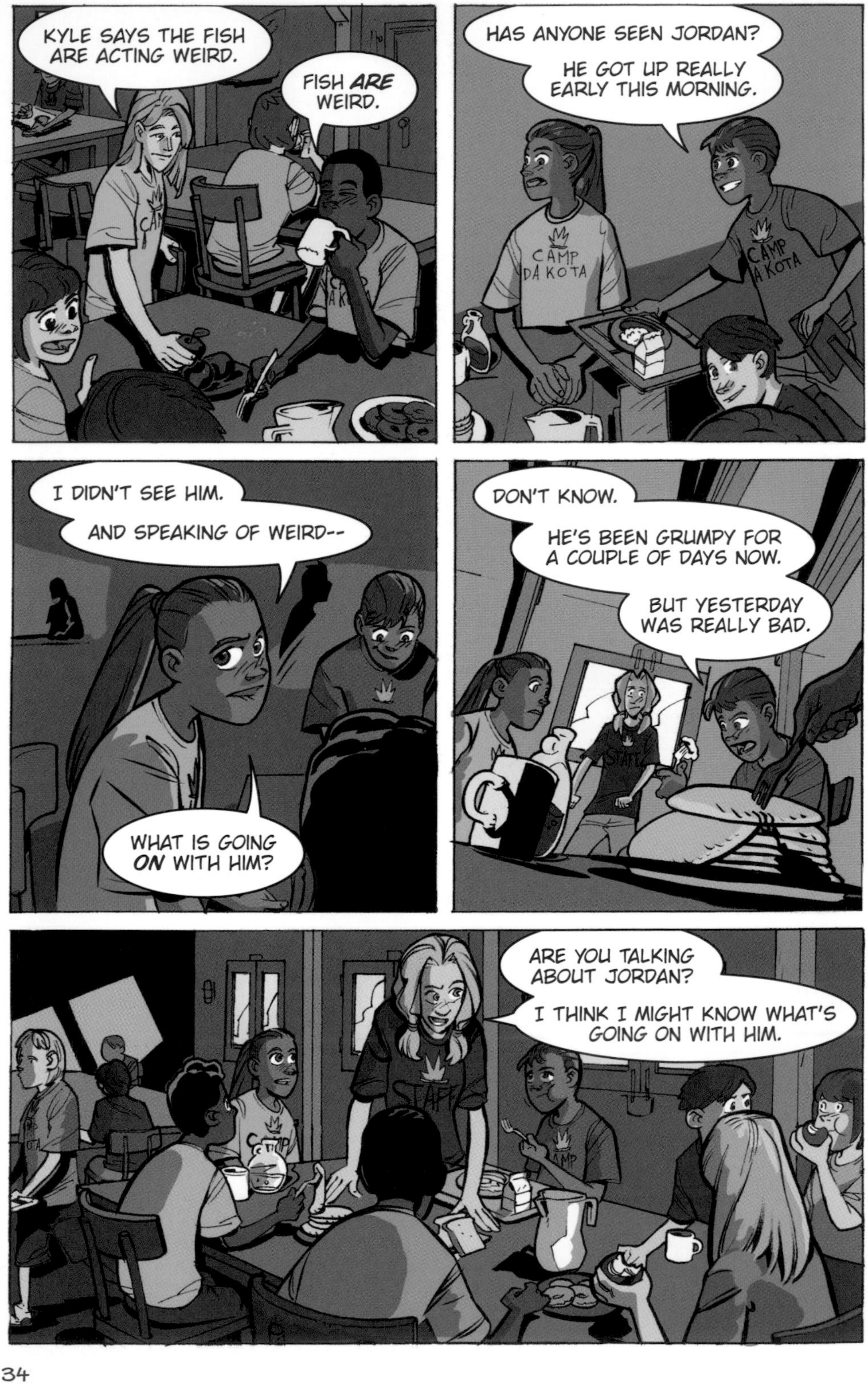
KYLE SAYS THE FISH ARE ACTING WEIRD.
FISH *ARE* WEIRD.
HAS ANYONE SEEN JORDAN?
HE GOT UP REALLY EARLY THIS MORNING.
CAMP DAKOTA
I DIDN'T SEE HIM.
AND SPEAKING OF WEIRD--
WHAT IS GOING *ON* WITH HIM?
DON'T KNOW.
HE'S BEEN GRUMPY FOR A COUPLE OF DAYS NOW.
BUT YESTERDAY WAS REALLY BAD.
ARE YOU TALKING ABOUT JORDAN?
I THINK I MIGHT KNOW WHAT'S GOING ON WITH HIM.

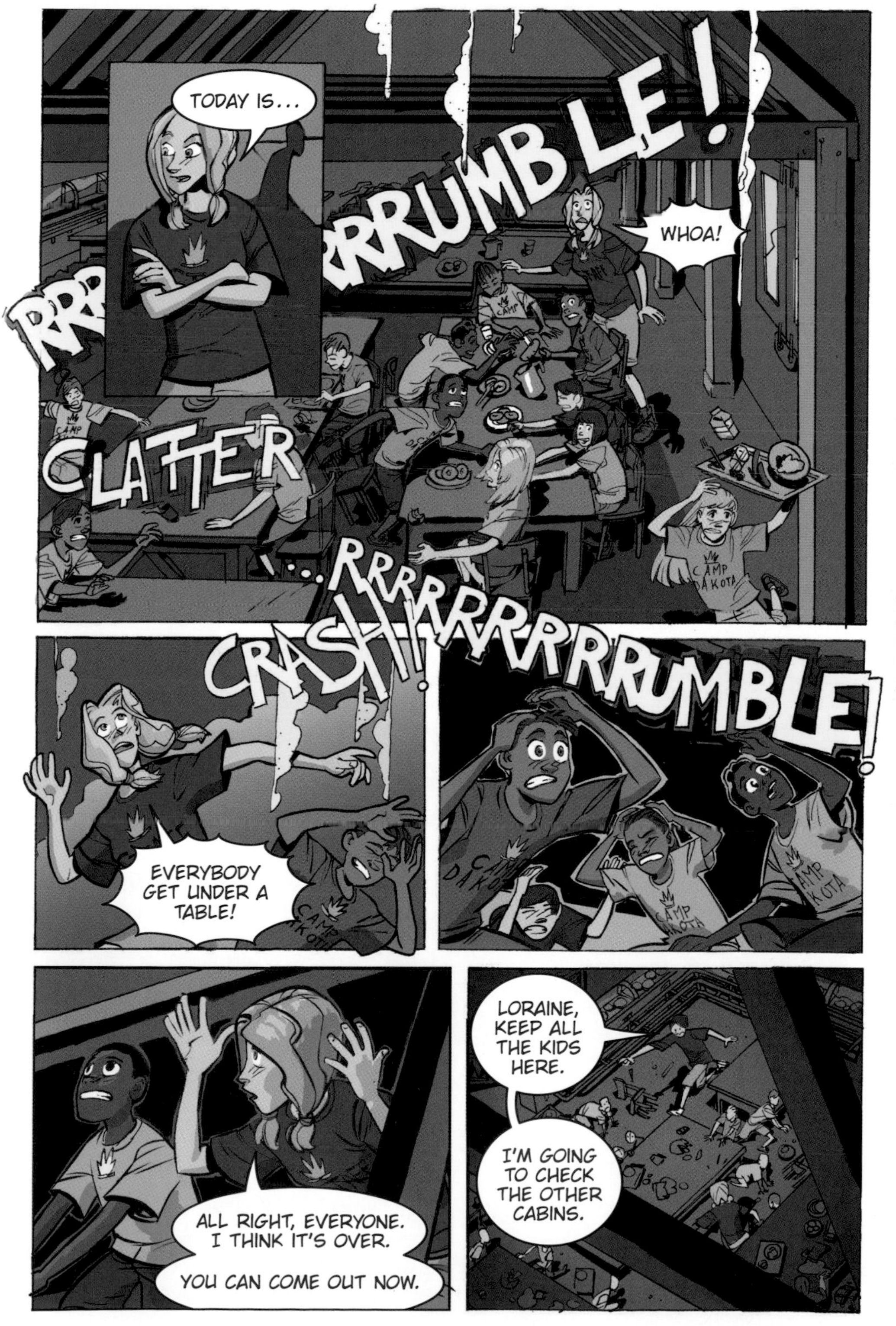
TODAY IS...
RRRRRUMBLE!
WHOA!
CLATTER
...RRRRRRRRRRUMBLE!
CRASH!
EVERYBODY GET UNDER A TABLE!
ALL RIGHT, EVERYONE. I THINK IT'S OVER.
YOU CAN COME OUT NOW.
LORAINE, KEEP ALL THE KIDS HERE.
I'M GOING TO CHECK THE OTHER CABINS.

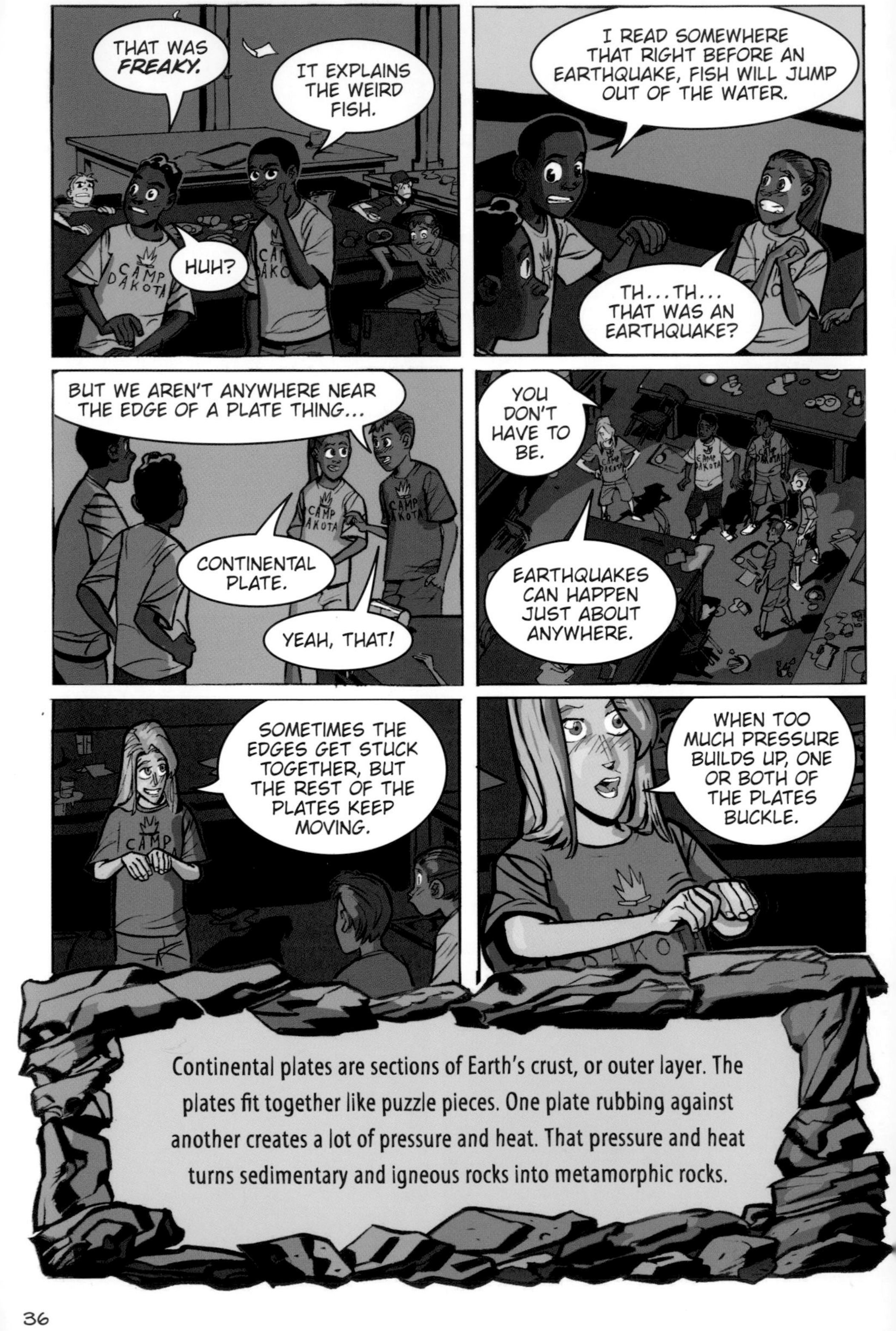
THAT WAS *FREAKY.*
IT EXPLAINS THE WEIRD FISH.
HUH?
I READ SOMEWHERE THAT RIGHT BEFORE AN EARTHQUAKE, FISH WILL JUMP OUT OF THE WATER.
TH...TH... THAT WAS AN EARTHQUAKE?
BUT WE AREN'T ANYWHERE NEAR THE EDGE OF A PLATE THING...
CONTINENTAL PLATE.
YEAH, THAT!
YOU DON'T HAVE TO BE.
EARTHQUAKES CAN HAPPEN JUST ABOUT ANYWHERE.
SOMETIMES THE EDGES GET STUCK TOGETHER, BUT THE REST OF THE PLATES KEEP MOVING.
WHEN TOO MUCH PRESSURE BUILDS UP, ONE OR BOTH OF THE PLATES BUCKLE.

Continental plates are sections of Earth's crust, or outer layer. The plates fit together like puzzle pieces. One plate rubbing against another creates a lot of pressure and heat. That pressure and heat turns sedimentary and igneous rocks into metamorphic rocks.

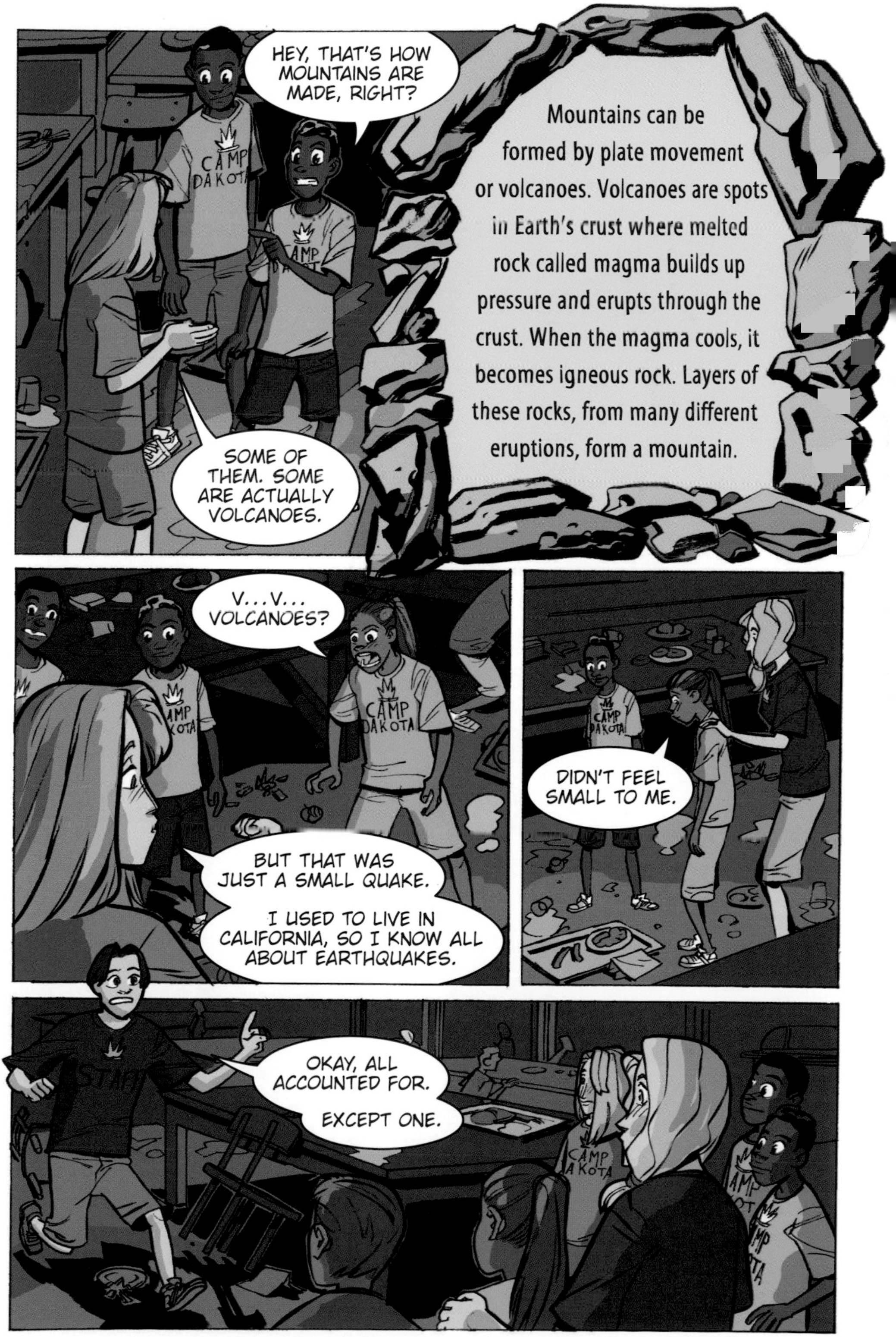
HEY, THAT'S HOW MOUNTAINS ARE MADE, RIGHT?
Mountains can be formed by plate movement or volcanoes. Volcanoes are spots in Earth's crust where melted rock called magma builds up pressure and erupts through the crust. When the magma cools, it becomes igneous rock. Layers of these rocks, from many different eruptions, form a mountain.
SOME OF THEM. SOME ARE ACTUALLY VOLCANOES.
V... V... VOLCANOES?
BUT THAT WAS JUST A SMALL QUAKE.
I USED TO LIVE IN CALIFORNIA, SO I KNOW ALL ABOUT EARTHQUAKES.
DIDN'T FEEL SMALL TO ME.
OKAY, ALL ACCOUNTED FOR.
EXCEPT ONE.

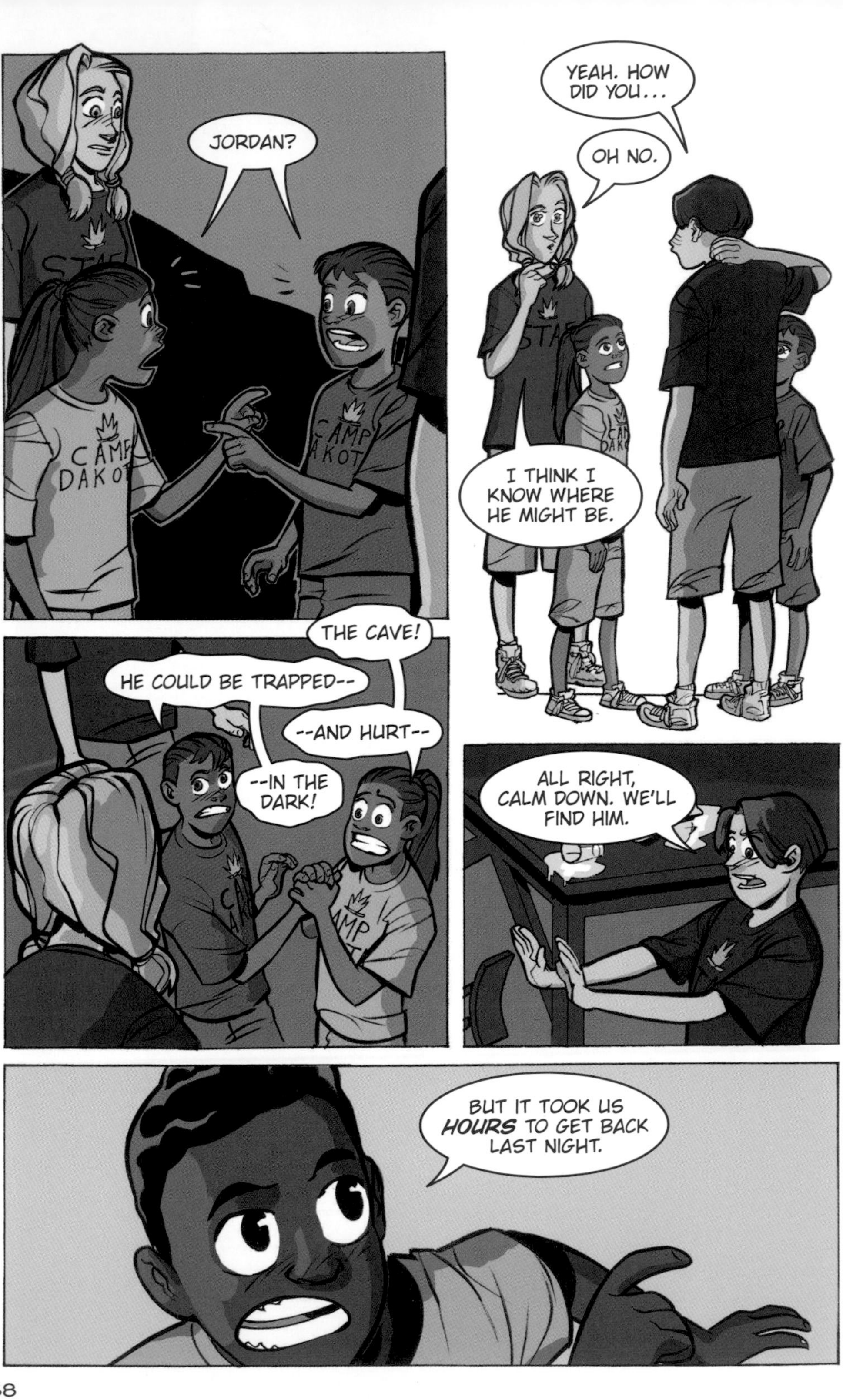
JORDAN?
YEAH. HOW DID YOU...
OH NO.
I THINK I KNOW WHERE HE MIGHT BE.
THE CAVE!
HE COULD BE TRAPPED--
--AND HURT--
--IN THE DARK!
ALL RIGHT, CALM DOWN. WE'LL FIND HIM.
BUT IT TOOK US ***HOURS*** TO GET BACK LAST NIGHT.

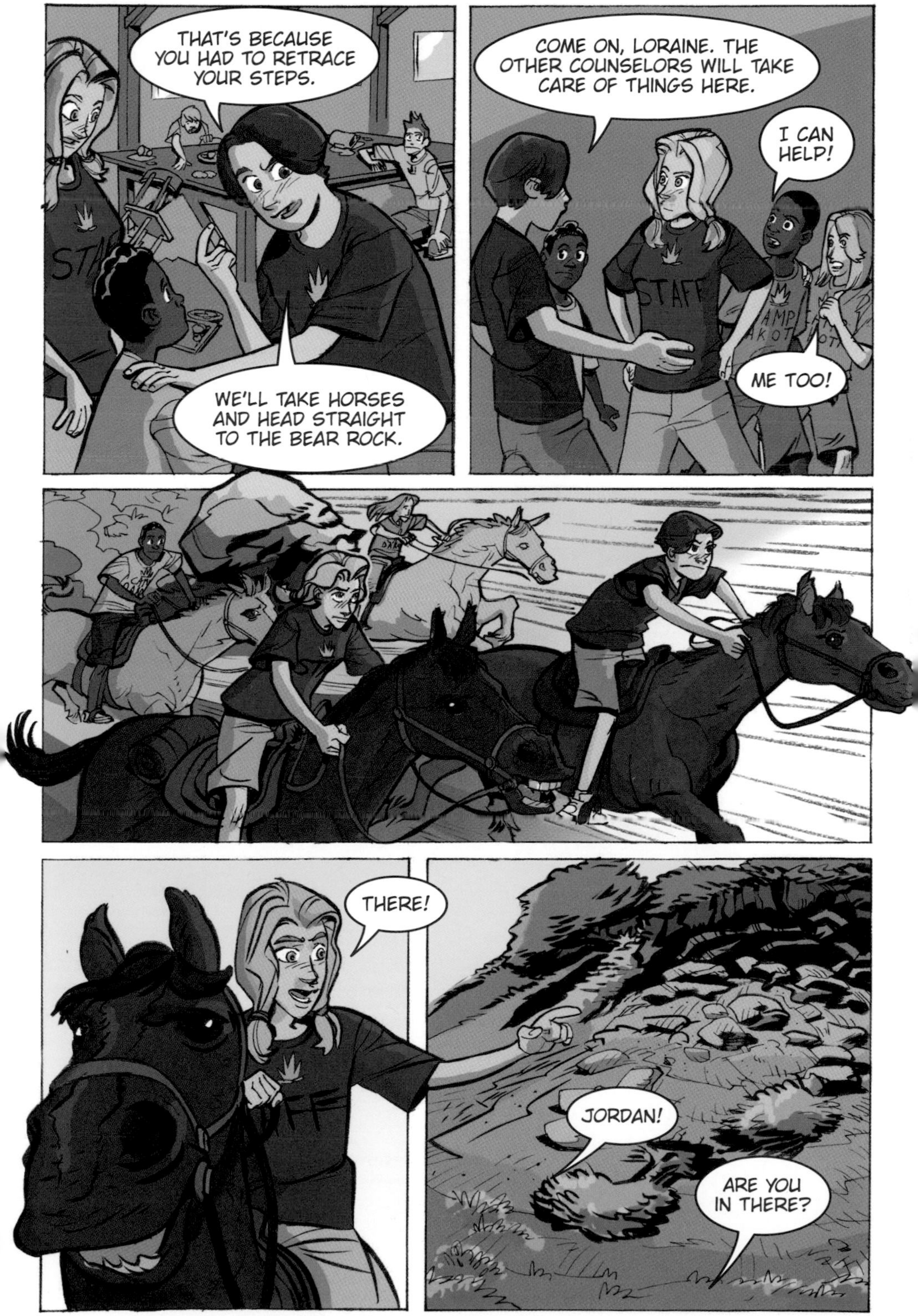
THAT'S BECAUSE YOU HAD TO RETRACE YOUR STEPS.
WE'LL TAKE HORSES AND HEAD STRAIGHT TO THE BEAR ROCK.
COME ON, LORAINE. THE OTHER COUNSELORS WILL TAKE CARE OF THINGS HERE.
I CAN HELP!
ME TOO!
THERE!
JORDAN!
ARE YOU IN THERE?

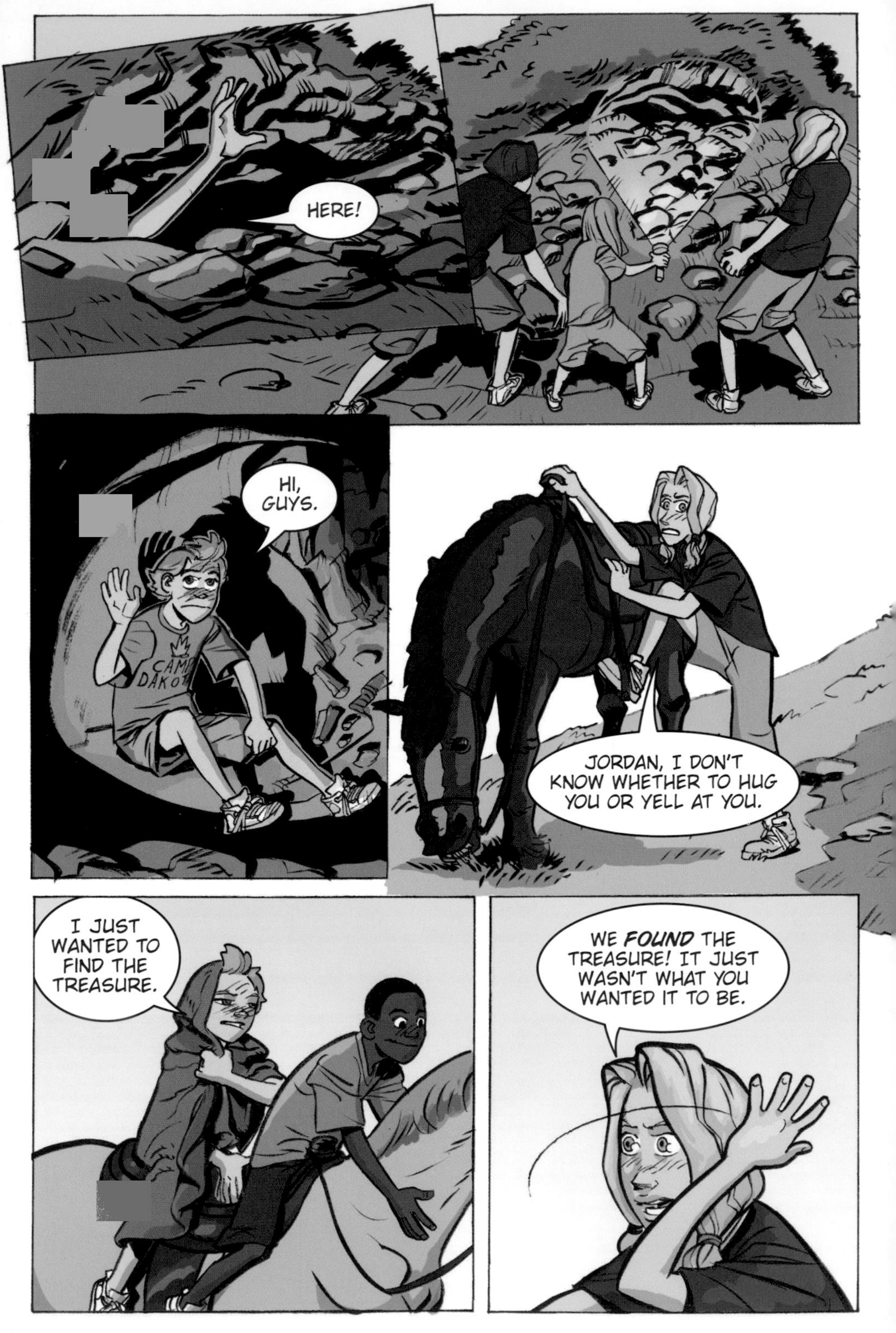
HERE!
HI, GUYS.
JORDAN, I DON'T KNOW WHETHER TO HUG YOU OR YELL AT YOU.
I JUST WANTED TO FIND THE TREASURE.
WE ***FOUND*** THE TREASURE! IT JUST WASN'T WHAT YOU WANTED IT TO BE.

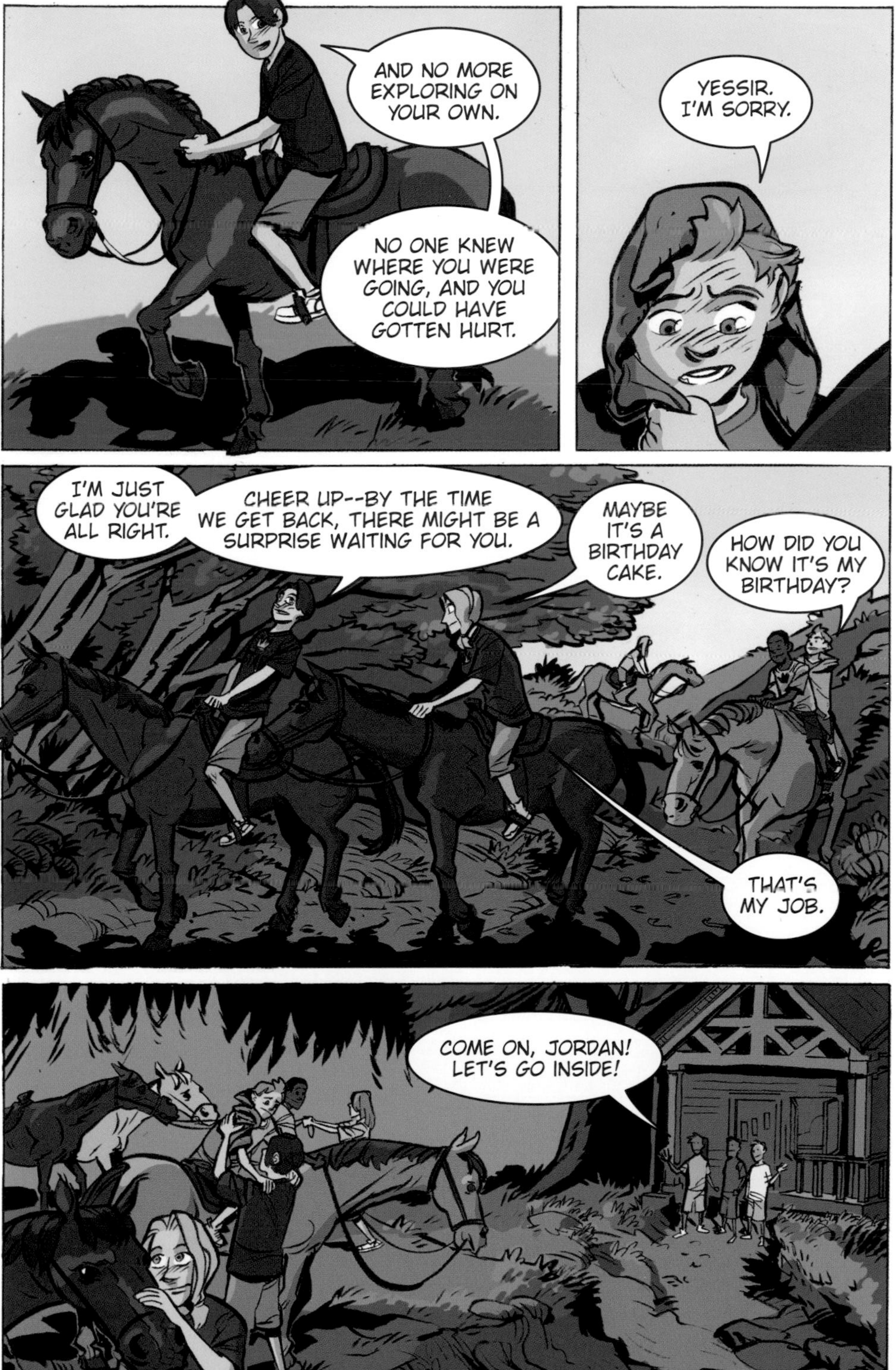
AND NO MORE EXPLORING ON YOUR OWN.
NO ONE KNEW WHERE YOU WERE GOING, AND YOU COULD HAVE GOTTEN HURT.
YESSIR. I'M SORRY.
I'M JUST GLAD YOU'RE ALL RIGHT.
CHEER UP--BY THE TIME WE GET BACK, THERE MIGHT BE A SURPRISE WAITING FOR YOU.
MAYBE IT'S A BIRTHDAY CAKE.
HOW DID YOU KNOW IT'S MY BIRTHDAY?
THAT'S MY JOB.
COME ON, JORDAN! LET'S GO INSIDE!

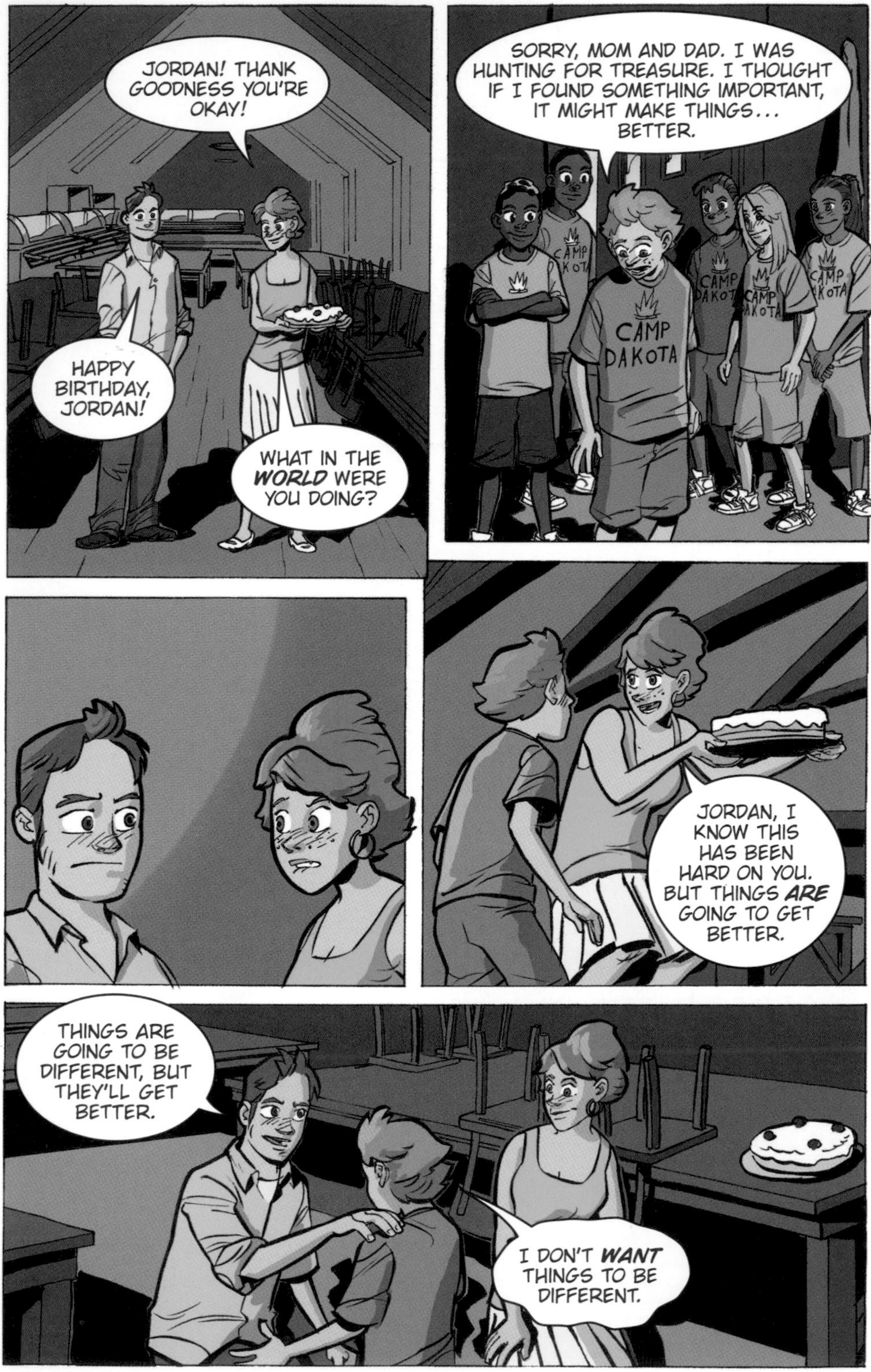
JORDAN! THANK GOODNESS YOU'RE OKAY!
HAPPY BIRTHDAY, JORDAN!
WHAT IN THE *WORLD* WERE YOU DOING?
SORRY, MOM AND DAD. I WAS HUNTING FOR TREASURE. I THOUGHT IF I FOUND SOMETHING IMPORTANT, IT MIGHT MAKE THINGS... BETTER.
CAMP DAKOTA
JORDAN, I KNOW THIS HAS BEEN HARD ON YOU. BUT THINGS *ARE* GOING TO GET BETTER.
THINGS ARE GOING TO BE DIFFERENT, BUT THEY'LL GET BETTER.
I DON'T *WANT* THINGS TO BE DIFFERENT.

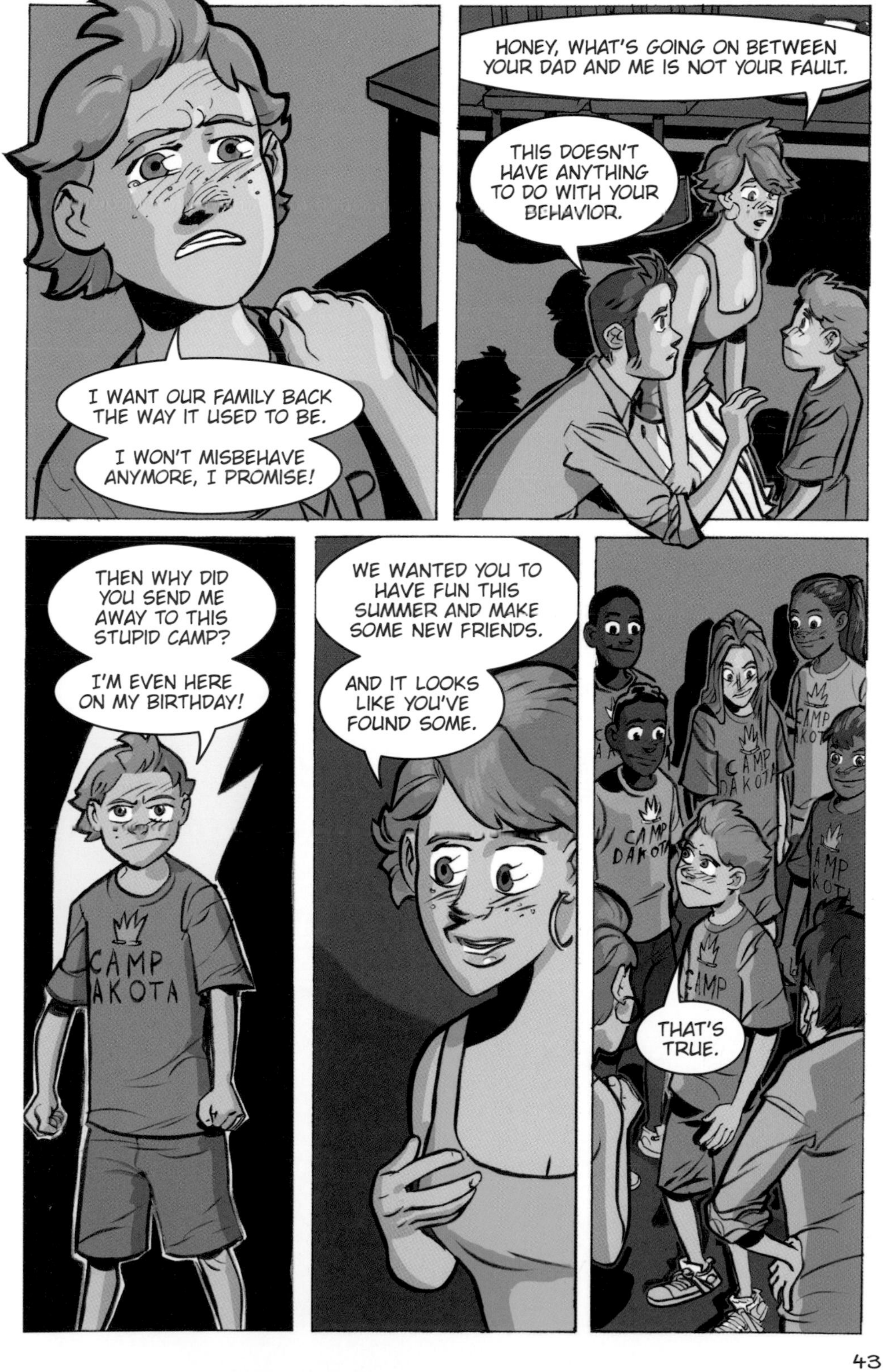
I WANT OUR FAMILY BACK THE WAY IT USED TO BE.
I WON'T MISBEHAVE ANYMORE, I PROMISE!
HONEY, WHAT'S GOING ON BETWEEN YOUR DAD AND ME IS NOT YOUR FAULT.
THIS DOESN'T HAVE ANYTHING TO DO WITH YOUR BEHAVIOR.
THEN WHY DID YOU SEND ME AWAY TO THIS STUPID CAMP?
I'M EVEN HERE ON MY BIRTHDAY!
CAMP DAKOTA
WE WANTED YOU TO HAVE FUN THIS SUMMER AND MAKE SOME NEW FRIENDS.
AND IT LOOKS LIKE YOU'VE FOUND SOME.
THAT'S TRUE.

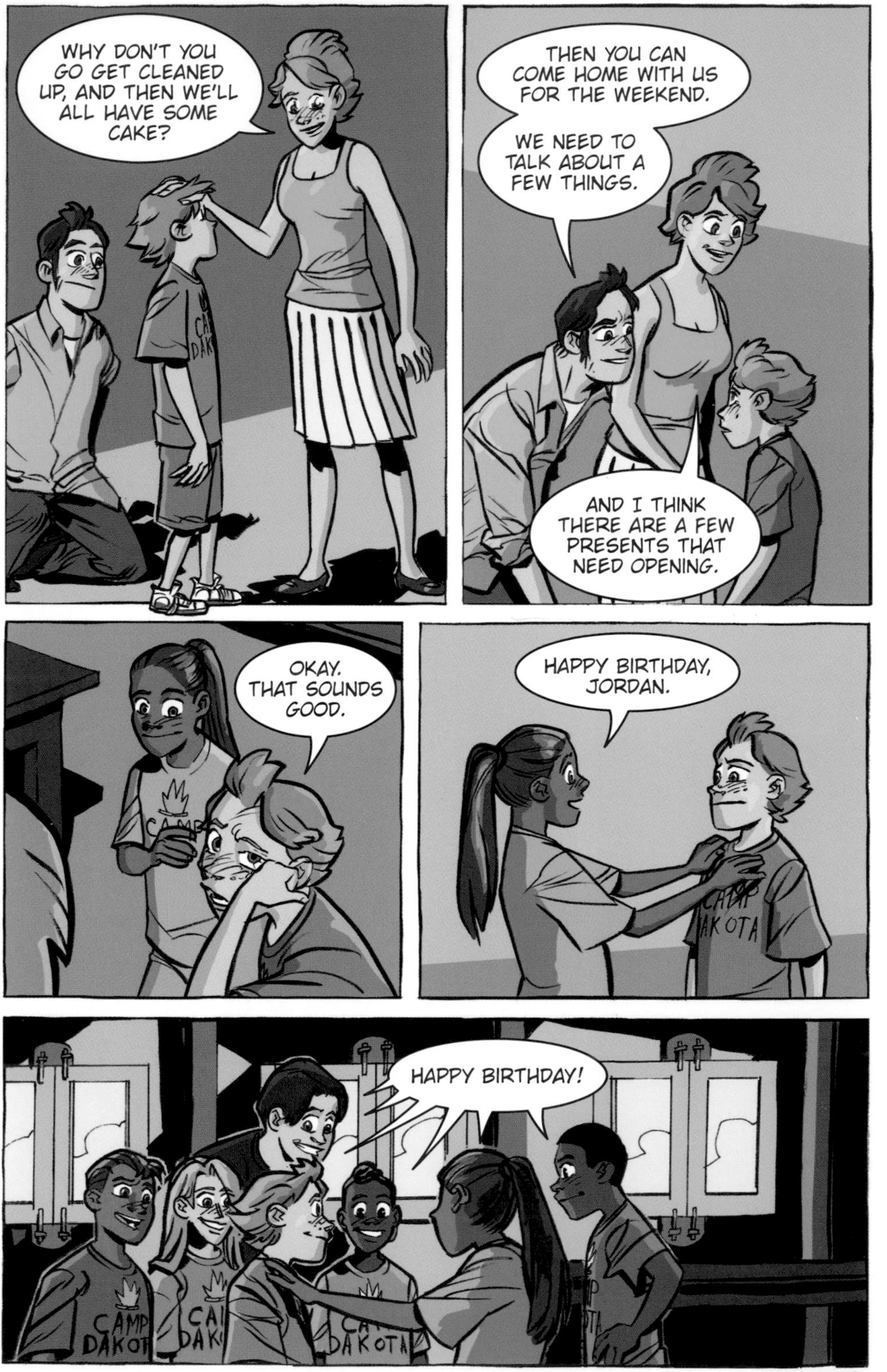
WHY DON'T YOU GO GET CLEANED UP, AND THEN WE'LL ALL HAVE SOME CAKE?
CAMP DAKOTA
THEN YOU CAN COME HOME WITH US FOR THE WEEKEND.
WE NEED TO TALK ABOUT A FEW THINGS.
AND I THINK THERE ARE A FEW PRESENTS THAT NEED OPENING.
OKAY. THAT SOUNDS GOOD.
HAPPY BIRTHDAY, JORDAN.
CAMP DAKOTA
HAPPY BIRTHDAY!
CAMP DAKOTA
DAKOTA

THE END

# Experiments

Try these fun experiments at home or in your classroom.
Make sure you have an adult help out.

## Sugar Glass

What you will need: cooking spray, baking sheet, small saucepan, ½ cup of sugar

1) Spray the baking sheet with cooking spray. Then put it in a freezer for an hour.

2) Put the sugar in the saucepan, and slowly heat it until it melts into a liquid, stirring constantly.

3) Take the baking sheet out of the freezer and pour the melted sugar on it.

4) Put the baking sheet back into the freezer for 10 minutes.

5) When you take it out of the freezer again, the sugar will have hardened into "glass."

### What happened?

Igneous rock is made up of minerals that melt in volcanoes, then cool quickly into rocks when they reach the much cooler surface. Sugar reacts similarly to heat and rapid cooling, changing from a crystalline solid, to a liquid, then into a "rock."

## Disappearing Act

What you will need: clear drinking glass, white chalk, vinegar

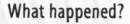

1) Put a piece of chalk in the drinking glass.

2) Fill the glass halfway with vinegar.

3) Watch as the chalk fizzes, starts to break up into smaller pieces, and finally disintegrates.

### What happened?

Chalk is made of calcite, a mineral in limestone. Vinegar is an acid. Calcite breaks down and changes into different substances when it reacts to acids. The bubbles are carbon dioxide gas.

Statues that are made of limestone are slowly worn down by weak acid rain.

# Mysterious Words

**acidic:** containing acids that can react to certain materials and produce salts

**calcite:** a common mineral found in limestone, marble, and chalk. It is also known as calcium carbonate.

**carbon dioxide:** a colorless, odorless gas. It is produced by respiration and fermentation, and is part of Earth's atmosphere.

**continental plate:** huge, thick plates of rock that make up Earth's outer layer

**decompose:** to break down or disintegrate into smaller parts or elements

**erosion:** the process by which Earth's surface is broken down and transported by wind, water, or glaciers

**igneous:** a type of rock that has been formed by molten rock that has cooled and hardened

**limestone:** sedimentary rock that is made up mostly of calcite. When combined with powdered clay, it makes cement.

**metamorphic:** a type of rock that forms deep below Earth's surface when other types of rock are changed by heat, pressure, and chemical reactions

**sediment:** matter that settles to the bottom of a liquid mixture; a mineral that is deposited by water, wind, or ice

**sedimentary:** a type of rock that is formed when shells, plants, and bones are pressed together

**weathering:** the process by which rocks are broken down by elements such as wind and water

# Could YOU have solved the Mystery of the Hidden Treasure?

Good thing the kids of Camp Dakota knew a bit about rocks and changes in Earth's surface—and got some helpful tips from the counselors. See if you caught all the facts they put to use.

- Wood can become a fossil over many years. When wood is buried under rocks and sand, water carries minerals from the rocks into the wood. The wood's living cells break down, leaving the minerals in their place. The result is called petrified wood.

- Erosion causes waterfalls to move over time. The flowing water carries rocks and soil from the top of the waterfall downstream. This moves the waterfall backward.

- Shells or skeletons of animals such as oysters can also become fossils. Sometimes these fossils appear far from where the animal lived, because glaciers carried them to a new place long ago.

- Weathering occurs when wind, water, plants, and animals break down rocks into smaller pieces. Unlike erosion, weathering doesn't move the smaller pieces—it just loosens them.

- A cave forms when water dissolves rock underground. Water becomes acidic by taking carbon dioxide from the air and dead plants. This acidic water seeps into the ground and into cracks in limestone rock below the soil. It erodes the limestone. The cracks grow bigger until they form a cave.

- Stalactites and stalagmites are the formations that hang from the ceiling and shoot up from the floor of a cave. They form when water carrying the mineral calcite drips from the ceiling. The water evaporates, leaving the calcite behind.

- Earthquakes can happen anywhere. They may occur far from the edge of a continental plate if pressure builds up within a plate whose edge is stuck against another plate edge.

# THE AUTHOR

**LYNDA BEAUREGARD** wrote her first story when she was seven years old and hasn't stopped writing since. She also likes teaching kids how to swim, designing websites, directing race cars out onto the track, and throwing bouncy balls for her cat, Becca. She lives near Detroit, Michigan, with her two lovely daughters, who are doing their best to turn her hair gray.

# THE ARTISTS

**DER-SHING HELMER** graduated from University of California—Berkeley, where she played with snakes and lizards all summer long. When she is not teaching biology to high school students, she is making art and comics for everyone to enjoy. Her best friends are her two pet geckos (Smeg and Jerry), her king snake (Clarice), and the chinchilla that lives next door.

**GUILLERMO MOGORRÓN** started drawing before he could walk or talk. When he is not drawing monsters or spaceships piloted by monkeys, he loves to fight with his cat and walk his dog. He also enjoys meeting friends and reading comics. He lives near Madrid, Spain.

**GERMAN TORRES** has always loved to draw. He also likes to drive his van to the mountains and enjoy a little fresh air with his girlfriend and dogs. But what he really loves is traveling. He lives in a town near Barcelona, Spain, away from the noise of the city.